A Bathory Universe Novel

Child OF THE Outcast

SPECIAL EDITION

Get bitten!

BORN VAMPIRE SERIES BOOK TWO

ELIZABETH DUNLAP

OTHER BOOKS BY ELIZABETH DUNLAP

Born Vampire Series: Ya Edition (Completed)

Knight of the Hunted (1)

Child of the Outcast (2)

War of the Chosen (3)

Bite of the Fallen (4)

Rise of the Monsters (5)

Time of the Ancients (6)

Born Vampire Series: NSFW Edition (Completed)

Knight of the Hunted (1)

Child of the Outcast (2)

War of the Chosen (3)

Bite of the Fallen (4)

Rise of the Monsters (5)

Time of the Ancients (6)

Born Vampire Short Stories

Tales of the Favored: Arthur's Tale (3.5)

Affairs of the Immortal: The Sinful Affair (4.4)

Affairs of the Immortal: The Knight and Arthur Affair (4.5)

Affairs of the Immortal: The Valentine's Day Affair (6.5)

This is a work of fiction. Names, characters, places, and incidents either are the product of the author's imagination or are used fictitiously, and any resemblance to any persons, living or dead, business establishments, events, or locales is entirely coincidental.

CHILD OF THE OUTCAST SPECIAL EDITION

Copyright © 2020 by Elizabeth Dunlap

First Printing: July, 2017

Printed in the United States of America

First Edition: July, 2017

❀ Created with Vellum

*Dedicated to my unfailingly faithful partner, Jesse.
A lot of the events in this book were taken from my own life, and now
that you're here, I never have to go through them again.*

INTRODUCTION

Dear readers,

As mentioned in the description, this is a slow build reverse harem paranormal romance. You may not see the harem for several books, but don't fret! It's definitely there!

If slow build isn't your thing, that's completely fine! But if you don't mind waiting a little for it, keep reading!

Sincerely,

Elizabeth Dunlap

DEAD INSIDE

I'd never felt such agony. Pure, debilitating agony.

That's what awaited me as Arthur dragged my lifeless body into the doors of the castle, past my peers who gave me more than a passing glance with their judgy faces, and to a halting stop at the staircase. I was so numb. Dead inside with grief, and so removed I didn't even care that the other vampires were whispering and staring at me. What did it matter? I didn't have the strength to feel shame.

I waited for the tug from Arthur at my bound wrists. He wasn't gentle. The skin under my binds was an angry red. If I was a human, there would be no skin left. I needed blood to heal, but since I had become his captive the week before, he gave me no more than a mouthful of gross bagged blood every morning. Any strength I'd had from it was slowly ebbing away like a fading tide.

"What have you done to her?" I heard Othello's indignant tone across the room where Arthur stood with him.

"She's a prisoner of the Council," Arthur's scratchy voice explained. "Her treatment isn't your concern."

Knight's beautiful perfect face washed before my eyes and I felt the sting of tears. Was he dead? Had they already judged him without first making sure he was as violent as they thought he was? Had he even been given a chance to plead for his own life? I couldn't picture his eyes dimming and his body going still. A small sliver of his lifeless corpse slipped into my mind and I felt my sanity fading away.

"What have they done to you?" Othello said again, this time much closer to my ears. I glanced upwards and barely registered that he was standing in front of me. He stunk of dead flowers, as usual. Gag.

"They took him," I murmured in a broken tone, and a sob escaped my lips. "They let him be taken away to die."

"Who, my pet?" He lifted a hand to stroke my hair but I shied away from him. "What is she talking about, Arthur?" he demanded.

Arthur didn't answer, probably deeming the information unnecessary. "Has the Council arrived?" he asked instead.

"Yes, they're all here. And they've begun the discussion of guilt."

Good. The sooner they decided my fate the better. I hoped they picked to execute me. I wanted to die. If Knight was dead, I wanted to die. Being banished would just mean I'd have to do it myself.

The conversation over, Arthur grabbed my restraints and started pulling me up the stairs. I stumbled several times as I wasn't focused on anything except my internal turmoil. Not even caring about me, he dragged me up the staircase and the restraints on my hand started cutting into my skin, dropping blood on the carpet. I caught my footing at the landing and followed Arthur down the dark red-carpeted hallway.

"You really know how to treat a gal," I mumbled halfway down the hall. He glanced at me and saw the blood coming from my wrists.

"You're a prisoner," he said evenly, uncaring with his stupid apathetic face.

"And you're a total douche," I retorted. "Funny how you have zero humanity. I bet you came out of your mother's womb and said, 'Hey mom, you deserved all that labor pain. Screw you.'" Maybe the pain was talking, or I needed to vent my anger. I knew how rude I was being, and I didn't give a hoot.

"If you were any other prisoner, I'd..." His jaw clenched, holding in the rest of the sentence.

"You'd what?" I stepped faster to catch up with him. "You'd slap me? Beat me? You've already proven you don't care about anyone but yourself." I tugged on my chains until he stopped walking. "How did they know where to find him? How, Arthur? Was it you? Did you tell the Lycans? Tipped them off for a sweet little payoff?"

"It wasn't like that," he ground out.

"You turned him in, you bastard. He did nothing to you

3

and you turned him in." He tried to move forward but I held tightly and more blood dripped from my bonds.

"He was dangerous."

I tugged again and again. The scent of blood was filling the air. "You didn't effing know that. The Council ordered you to find me, not him. You *decided* to turn Knight in, because you hate everything. You could've just let him go, but why the hell would you want to do that?"

That icy blue stare turned to me, and he unclenched his jaw enough to speak. "He was dangerous," Arthur repeated.

Pulling on the chain, I moved closer to my captor until we were almost chest to chest. I could smell him and it made me sick. My purple eyes glared at his cold chiseled face.

"*I'm* dangerous," I informed him.

He looked away and without me holding him back, he continued walking down the hall. When he stopped again, he unlocked a familiar door and unlocked my chains before shoving me inside and slamming the door in my face. I placed a hand on the white wood of the door. The lock had been changed and the security chains removed. This door no longer locked from the inside.

I was a prisoner. A prisoner in my own rooms.

All my hatred and rage settled on the figure outside of my door. I pressed my mouth to the crack between the frame.

"You killed him and you didn't have to. Never forget that." My legs slowly folded and I slumped against the door in a broken heap.

I had become a criminal for sparing a child's life. A Lycan

child, but still a child. Even now, after all that had happened, I didn't regret what I'd done. My only regret was that Knight would be killed for my mistakes. The solitude constantly reminded me that Knight was probably dead by now, and my sorrow slowly carved out a deep well of emotion I couldn't climb out of.

I didn't move from my spot at the door for hours. Every movement outside my door made me jump, waiting for Arthur to burst in and drag me back downstairs for sentencing. He never did. Was he sitting on the floor too, or did he get a chair for his psycho butt? Maybe he should put up a tent so we wouldn't have to look at his douchy face.

The second day was harder. I slept by the door and woke up cramped and hungry. My wrists were still damaged, the skin peeling in some areas. I could barely feel the pain but it was making me so thirsty.

At 8 am on the dot, Arthur opened the door and tossed in a bag of blood like I was an animal in a cage. He quickly shut it again and locked it. Outside the door, I heard him talking to whoever had brought the blood. I was too thirsty to pay attention and dove for the bag, tearing into it and slurping up every drop the plastic had to offer. As soon as the blood hit my stomach, I felt a wave of nausea and then my wrists started to heal. Losing blood to fix the injury made me thirstier than I was before. Prisoners didn't deserve a companion, I guessed. My muscle mass was already receding. Living on Knight's blood had made me the strongest I'd ever been. Now I felt weak and helpless.

I slid the empty blood bag under the door and lay spread eagle on the entryway carpet, staring up at the vaulted ceiling. No popcorn ceilings in this castle, no sir. Everything was perfection. It was all a façade. A lie. A smoke screen to make you think we lived a perfect immortal life.

I hated this castle, and everything it represented. It represented a society that outcast me for sparing a child. A society that sent a Hunter after me who thought killing my boyfriend was okay.

Sweet, beautiful Knight. I'll never see your face again.

The door opened again and Arthur stood with a tray of food. I looked up at him from the carpet and lifted my middle finger for his appraisal. He laid the tray down next to me and shut the door again, flipping the locks like they owed him money. Without getting up, I felt at the tray's contents with my fingers and lifted bite after bite of eggs, bacon, and biscuits to my mouth until it was empty.

The passage of time barely registered and it seemed like I'd just eaten breakfast when Arthur opened the door again. He picked up the empty tray and replaced it with one that had my lunch on it. His job done, he stood in the doorway watching me. I was still staring up at the ceiling. I wasn't in the mood to look at him.

"If you ask if I'm okay, I swear to god, I will stab you with a pencil," I spat in his direction.

"Your wellbeing is inconsequential." I scoffed out a laugh. "I am, however, tasked with making sure you stay alive until your trial."

That made me look over at him. "Trial? Oh, isn't that fancy. I get a trial. Is it a trial by fire? That would be *perfect*. I plan on going up in flames any way."

"As I said, I am tasked with keeping you alive." He dipped his chin at me and I understood what he was getting at.

"Ahh. Wouldn't want me killing myself before you can execute me. Cute. Didn't know you cared." I looked down at the tray and saw it was a bowl of chili with enough peppers to kill your taste buds. I pushed it towards his foot and turned away again.

"Eat," he commanded, toeing the food my way. Some of the chili spilled out onto the tray.

"I don't like peppers. If I am to have any sort of freedom, I will not eat what I don't enjoy. You can eat it, I don't care. Now go away."

Bending, he took the tray and left, and I was free again to get lost in my musings. When I wasn't picturing Knight's dead body, I relived every moment of my time under James's control. How he'd held me close to him and I'd felt so helpless. I'd never let anyone make me feel that way again. And sweet Sara. During my blood binge, I had become her abuser, ordering her around like a servant. I felt like a traitor. I'd fought so hard to protect humans and I'd mistreated one. I hoped she could forgive me for my abuse.

Days were marked only by the sunlight returning after darkness. I was beginning to creep up to the edges of my sanity. How long would I be in here waiting? I'd never been a patient person, and this tested every bit of resolve I had. I just had to wait it out. Soon, any day now, Arthur would come to get me, and the Council would find me guilty. I had to hold onto that hope.

The carpet was my only friend. If I moved away from the door, I wouldn't be able to hear anything outside. Days passed, and the only interruption from the ceiling was Arthur bringing blood and food, and the occasional trip to the bathroom.

I'd cried so many times, I could no longer cry. I simply lay there, thinking about Knight dying because of me. He didn't deserve any of this.

"How long has it been?" I asked when Arthur emerged again, holding a dinner tray that he set beside me.

"Two weeks," he answered. Hell. Two weeks already. What was taking so long? "You smell rank. I suggest a shower before you start merging with the carpet."

"If we're on the subject of rankness, you haven't showered in two weeks either. Don't think I can't smell it. The stink has been creeping under the door for days."

He was gone before I could start throwing my food at him. He'd learned early on that I cared more about making him suffer than eating, plus I had a good throwing arm, and seeing him with a canned peach on his face was hilarious. Annoyingly, he was right though. I smelled bad. It was time to leave the carpet.

I got up, stretched, and took a two hour bath. Maybe the water would wash away more than dead skin and carpet fibers. Finally clean, I put on a robe and wandered around from room to room. I stood in Cameron's old room, and seeing it empty made me feel even worse. I pressed my face into the carpet, hoping against hope I could catch his scent just so I could feel better for a few seconds. Alas, the carpet had been shampooed after he moved out, and no trace scent remained.

Was he happy?

Cameron deserved a full and happy life. I wanted it for him more than I wanted almost anything else, beyond to see Knight again, and maybe sucker punch James a few times. I didn't expect happiness in my life again, so I wanted it for Cameron that much more.

If he was living a good life, I could find a little bit of comfort.

2

A CRAPPY JAILER

The days were beginning to blur together. The only marker of time passing was the consistent supply of bagged blood every morning and the trays of food. I often wondered if Arthur should just install a doggie door to slip the food and blood into, so then he would never have to unlock my door. At least my cell was nicely decorated and had working plumbing. It was achingly lonely being in solitary confinement. Even someone like me, who didn't thrive on social interaction, was hitting my limit. I would've traded my blood ration for the chance to see someone other than my own reflection and Arthur's stupid face.

I wasn't the type to talk to myself, so I didn't even have myself to interact with. The silence was noisier than a busy sidewalk. Arthur, the jerk, had taken my phone, and with it my music, so I couldn't immerse myself in Copeland or

Tchaikovsky. I couldn't sing along with Gershwin or show tune it up with Sondheim. He might as well have taken all my books away. I did at least have those to escape into, and it was quite literally the only comfort I had once I stopped lying on the carpet. With nothing else to do, I went through at least two or three books a day, diving into Narnia and building the pyramids brick by brick.

I still sat by the door while I read. I was never far away from it. When I'd gone through a nice chunk of my very large book collection, I decided to take action. Was I truly without rights? I wrote up a note of things I'd like to be purchased with my credit card and quickly slipped it under the door around the time I knew Arthur would be giving me my bag of blood.

He slipped it back under, because of course he would.

"Jerk," I complained to the door.

"I'm not buying you makeup," he retorted. Oh, so he could actually hear me. He'd just been choosing to ignore me this entire time. He was such an a-hole.

"You didn't even look at the list, butt face. I want new books to read, I'm almost out of shampoo, and I can't do my laundry in here. Is your prisoner supposed to run out of clean underwear?"

He sighed and I heard him scratching at his face. "Fine. Slip it back under." I did, and listened to him opening the paper. "You put 'I'll pay 1,000 euros if someone will strangle Arthur' on the second page."

"Feel free to post that around the castle," I said sweetly.

"You really want to live without clean underwear, don't you?" He shoved the note back without my credit card. Great. He'd probably run up my bill buying dirty magazines.

I laid down on one of my couches and fell asleep. Lilacs drifted into my dreams. The scent woke me up and I saw Balthazar sitting at my feet. I sat up and fell into his arms. As I held him to me, I realized I needed him now more than ever.

"Don't leave," I begged him, clutching him close. "I'm so alone. Please don't leave."

I could feel him smile against my shoulder. "You don't want me here all the time, pet. It would get very boring."

"I don't care. I need you. You never stay when I need you."

"I know," he admitted gently, running his fingers through my hair. "I'll stay. Not all the time, but I'll be here as often as I can."

I gripped his fancy suit jacket and his long black hair in my hands, reassuring myself that he was actually here and not a figment of my loneliness. "More often than once a month?"

"As often as I can," he promised. He pushed me away and fussed with my black curls. The perm and coloring I'd gotten had faded, and I was back to my natural beautiful hair. "I'm sorry I couldn't come sooner. I was busy."

"Copenhagen?" I teased with our private joke. "If so, can I have some juicy details? I'm a bit starved of companionship."

"Sorry to disappoint, but you are the only woman in my life." Balthazar leaned over and kissed me on the forehead.

Did he really mean that?

I looked up at him, almost hopeful. "You know things, right? Is Knight..." I couldn't say the word 'dead' even if I'd been picturing it over and over so many times it was burned into my retinas.

Balthazar had never lied to me, so I believed him when he said, "They won't let him live, Lisbeth." If I hadn't been in solitude for three weeks, constantly reminding myself of the truth he'd just spoken, I would've broken in half. I would've lost it. Instead, I sat there and felt everything go numb, like a block of ice was crawling all over me. His arms pulled me into a soothing hug. "I'm so sorry, my love," he murmured. "I wish I could spare you this pain. I'd take it from you in a heartbeat if it was possible."

The tone in his voice spoke of a time when he felt what I was feeling. Had he lost my mother? My grandmother? Which one caused him that pain? Who had broken his heart? It was more than comforting to be with someone who knew my pain. I didn't want to let Balthazar go. I held him until I couldn't feel my arms anymore. And then, I fell asleep against his neck.

As my confinement went on and on like a merry-go-round, I began to wonder what was happening. What was taking the Council so damn long? Maybe they were busy with other things and were putting my trial off because screw that law breaking chick and her problems. I wished I knew.

Balthazar's visits were odd and amazing all at once. I'd never seen this much of him in all my four hundred years. Not ever. We played games, sat together reading books, played on my piano, and painted pictures of each other.

It helped take my mind off the pain. But it couldn't erase it. Nothing could. Vampires never forgot anything. I'd always feel with blinding clarity how much it hurt to lose Knight. Over time, it would move to the back of my mind, but it would always be there lurking in the shadows, waiting for a weak moment to jump out again. Something to look forward to.

About two weeks after I'd given Arthur the list, I was running dangerously low on clean clothes. He opened the door for breakfast, he was always punctual so I knew when to be ready. In one hand he held my tray and I reached for it to set it down. In the other hand he held a bottle of men's all-in-one shampoo.

You are kidding me.

"Laundry please," he said, and held out the bottle for me to take.

I hauled my overloaded hamper to him and curled my nose at the shampoo bottle. "That's for men." He looked me dead in the eyes and dropped it on the carpet before picking the hamper up and leaving. "YOU'RE LITERALLY THE WORST!!" I shouted at the door.

He returned my clothes the next day, as wrinkled as an old lady's double chin.

15

Time was passing like a slow crawl and a giant leap all at once. Arthur continued to make my confined life as difficult as possible. His stupid all-in-one shampoo was making my hair a rat's nest. It was a blessing I wasn't in mixed company looking like a frumpy mess of curls.

When I'd been confined for seven weeks, Olivier barged into my room followed by a complaining Arthur. I hadn't seen her, or anyone from the castle, since I'd been brought back. Her long dreads had been cropped short to her head leaving behind very short curls, and she was wearing a plain black dress. I guessed I wasn't the only one who had changed recently. She was carrying a small birdcage and handed me a tiny baby bird.

"Cameron found it," she told me once it was in my hand.

"You're not allowed in here, Olivier," Arthur complained behind her. She flipped him off and rolled her eyes where only I could see.

"It probably has lice or rabies or whatever birds get. Have fun." She smiled and gave me a little finger wave before leaving the way she came. Arthur fumed in the doorway once she was gone.

"I'm not feeding it for you," he proclaimed, crossing his arms over his chest.

I opened the little bird cage and put the baby bird inside. It couldn't have been more than a few days old, its skin patchy with little down feathers. It looked as helpless as I felt. "If I'm executed, you won't have to." I sunk down onto the carpet and watched the little bird try to move around in the cage. It stumbled several times, but it was adorable to look at.

"Fine. I'll bring food for it." I looked up at him in confusion and he had relaxed his stance in the doorway. "What do they eat? Bugs?"

"I don't know. Look it up, since you have my phone." I wiggled a finger in between the bars and the baby looked up at me with its enormous eyes. The door shut, the locks flipped, and I smelled lilacs.

"What a cute little bird," Balthazar commented, suddenly sitting beside me.

"You're going to scare it if you keep doing that," I told him, only mildly serious.

He stuck his tongue out at me, and then he brought a hand up to pet my hair, sending soothing tingles all over me. "How are you?"

I looked down at the birdcage and sighed. "I hate being in here. I'm tired of wondering what the Order has decided, my fate constantly in the balance. And Knight." My voice faltered. "I'm trying to accept that he's gone. I am. I know he's dead and I'll never see him again."

"Stop." There was understanding and sympathy in his crystal blue eyes. "You loved him. Don't try to push yourself to move on. You need to grieve."

I tried to be brave. It was so hard after so long. "It's not the first time I've lost someone."

He sighed and kissed me on the forehead, gently and with so much love. "Yes, it is."

I wrapped my arms around him, the man who understood me so well. "Don't leave," I begged him.

"I won't," he promised.

BECOMING A DOLPHIN

This must be what Dolphins feel like. Those creatures of the sea are used to swimming for miles every day, and humans pen them up in little tanks they can't leave. How do they survive? How are they not crushed with sorrow every day? They can't be free anymore. They can't live.

I wished I could drown myself. That's what dolphins do when they don't want to live anymore. They just go under the water and never come back up. Stupid dolphins, having the ability to make themselves die. I envied them.

Dying would be a release. I wouldn't have to feel all this pain anymore. It would end with my last breath, and I'd fade into solace unknown.

The hot water of my bath swirled around my nose and ears, and I blinked to invite it under my eyes too. Let every last bubble of air escape my lungs. Would I die? Or would I just lie here in the water in stasis until my blood supply ran out from keeping me alive, and I woke with a red-eyed frenzy.

Something dark walked into the room and sat on the edge of my tub. I re-surfaced and wiped the water from my eyes.

"What the hell are you doing?" The voice I heard was Knight's. That was impossible, of course, so I knew I was hallucinating. Low on air, low on blood, boom. Imaginary dead boyfriend.

"I was being a dolphin," I informed him matter-of-factly. My delusions should be more well-informed. It was nice to see him, at any rate. Even if he was just a fantasy. It didn't give me the relief I hoped it would, but it was nice. His hair was greasy and his clothes messy like he'd rolled in a puddle. "You look like you need a bath more than I do," I said jokingly.

He sighed wearily. "Don't I know it." He surveyed the large tub around me. "Looks like that seats two. Mind if I joined?"

I scrunched my knees to my chest. "No way! You're not getting my bath water all dirty!"

He chuckled into his hand, his deep brown eyes studying me. "It's good to see you, Lis."

I turned my face away from the mirage. "You're not even here." When I blinked and looked back, he was gone.

I understood my delusion wasn't real. Knight hadn't visited me. It didn't fill me with hope for his survival, and it didn't relieve my pain. Plus, he'd ruined a perfectly good science experiment on vampires and drowning.

Did my trip to psycho land make me feel better? No. Was I going to keep pretending to be a dolphin so he would come back? Also no. I already felt my sanity slipping, and I didn't want it to get worse. Of course, being locked up was much worse than having delusions, and I began to lose hope that I would ever be let out. I'd just be here forever with Arthur outside the door denying me access to new books. I could only read my collection so many times before they became boring, and I was reaching that point.

Sometimes I tried to conjure Knight up again, but it never worked. I'd sit next to my little bird cage and picture him beside me. He never came. He was dead. A corpse. Gone. Forever. I'd never see his beautiful eyes or feel his gentle kisses.

I stopped feeling anything. Everything inside me was shattered. Pieces of me were all over the floor, little bits of Lisbeth. The bits that made me sane. They're scattered everywhere and I can't put them back together. There's only the bird, Arthur, and me.

"Lisbeth," someone said above me. I looked up to see the icy blue eyes. Go away, ice. I'm already frozen in time. "Your room is a mess," he said in disgust.

"What's the point, icy eyes? It's only me and this room. Can you see the pieces around me? I'm broken. Shattered."

The bird cheeped a few times and a tear fell down my face. "There is no world outside this room."

"Damn it," icy eyes said under his breath. He roughly pulled me up and I went limp like a dolly. "When was the last time you bathed?"

I laughed. "I don't remember. But I went underwater. Dolphins have it so easy. Bloop bloop." I reached out and tapped my finger against his nose. "Boop."

"Where's your friend?" he asked me, looking around at all the pieces of me, scattered all over the room.

"Friend? What friend? You're not my friend." I poked him in the chest this time and felt woozy, like I was going to fall forward against him.

"The one that smells like lilacs." Well knock me backwards. Bloodhound Arthur knew everything.

"Nothing gets past you, captor of mine. He's been gone for weeks. Jerk always bails on me. Piece of crap. Can't trust him with anything."

Arthur walked me over to the couch and pushed some pieces of me off before planting me on the cushions. "You're acting weird."

"*You're* weird," I countered. "I've been locked in this hell hole for months, you think my sanity is going to survive that? Since I've been in here, I've read every book I own five times, Arthur. Five. I have over 1,000 books. Let that sink into your tiny little butt brain. All my DVDs have been watched more times that I can count. I've painted on every canvas I have, and now I'm out of paper. And you still think that bringing me Men's All-in-One shampoo every month is all I need. You're such a jerk. If I didn't hate you for turning Knight in, I'd hate you because your people skills are zero, and lucky me gets to experience that first hand."

He sat down beside me, like little Miss Muffet. "You're acting like you're drunk."

"I wish I was effing drunk. I'd give anything to go outside. To open my windows and feel fresh air and sunlight. But no, you boarded them up like the stupid face you are." I crossed my arms over my chest, but it didn't work very well, it looked like I was feeling myself up.

"I'll try to get you some new books," he offered blankly, like nothing I'd said had gotten through to him. Not that I was surprised.

"If you think that can rescue my sanity, go ahead." I looked over at him and snarled.

"Need help cleaning up?"

I flipped him off. "Don't offer if you're not going to do it." He growled, got up, and walked to the door. "Arthur." His boots stopped right as he was reaching for the doorknob. "You're the only person I have right now. I know you're prob-ably not used to someone relying on you for all of their needs, but you're doing a pretty bad job. I'm not a goldfish you can simply feed and then ignore for the rest of the day. Funny how this is your job, taking care of prisoners, and you suck at it."

He rested his hand on the doorknob, not twisting it. "None of the others were given a trial. The only thing I had to do before was hide a body." Then he was gone.

My imprisonment had already reached the triple digits, according to Arthur. Even after our conversation, his idea of taking better care of me was better shampoo and one new book. It was 'Sun Tzu's The Art of War' and I briefly contemplated hitting him over the head with it before giving it back. It's not exactly a page turner.

When I felt as if my sanity was finally coming back to me, Cameron came in with my lunch one day.

"Sorry I didn't come sooner," he said after Arthur had shut and locked the door. "There was a Snorlax blocking the way."

"You're such a weirdo." I stopped mid-laugh and my heart stopped. I'd been in such a rush to run and hug him that I almost didn't notice that he was different.

Cameron wasn't human anymore.

I clasped a hand over my mouth to hold in the scream of sorrow I felt rising up my throat.

No.

Not him.

He was supposed to leave this hellhole and live his life. Find a girlfriend, get married, have annoying kids that liked video games. And die. He was supposed to die. Die a happy old man with his family at his side bidding him farewell in a bittersweet moment as he relived his beautiful happy life.

The hand over my mouth didn't stop me from crying.

"Why," I shouted between my gut-wrenching sobs. "Why did you become one of the turned? God damn it, Cameron.

Why did you do that? You were..." I cried harder, trying to get my words out. "You were supposed to have a life! A family! You weren't supposed to be frozen!"

"Lisbeth," he said gently over my wails. "Please let me explain." I quieted myself to broken sniffles and reached for a tissue to clean my face. He sighed at the sight of me and ran a hand through his newly dyed black locks. "When I came to you, I was a homeless teenager. I'd never slept somewhere for more than a few nights. I never had a home or a family. You gave me both. You raised me, and you became my friend, but we mean more to each other than just friends. You're my family. My onee-san[1], my big sister. I won't walk away from you. I used to think that what I wanted was to leave and get as far away from here as I could. Only, I was wrong. I want this life. I want to be with my sister. With you."

My lip shook. My hands shook. Everything shook. "But you were supposed to have a happy life as a human. That's what I wanted for you. I clung to that hope when I left here."

"I know. I know you wanted that for me, and I did too at first, but this is what I want now. Can you accept that?" I nodded and ran a hand across my eyes. "I'm sorry I hurt you," he apologized.

I studied his face with a sniff. "You're happy like this?" He nodded. "It's a Cardinal."

He looked confused. "What?"

"The baby bird. It's a Cardinal." I motioned towards the birdcage sitting on one of my end tables. The bird was sitting in the light of a lamp on its little perch inside the cage, and I could swear it was smiling with happiness as it chirped a little tune.

Cameron beamed when he saw the tiny bird. "It's still alive! Olivier didn't tell me if the little guy had made it. She's been too busy making kissy face with Renard."

Oh my god. I was more shocked than I would've been if he'd suddenly declared mad passionate love for me. It was even more shocking than him turning up in my room a newly turned vampire, or Knight showing up in my bathroom unannounced, or Arthur buying me shampoo that's actually for curls.

"Back up, sister. You said what now?"

He was trying not to laugh at my face. "Olivier. Renard. Sitting in a tree."

"Olivier is with a human?" I mean, he'd been her companion for thirty years now when almost every companion left after the obligatory ten. But still. He was a human. That was considered about as taboo as being with a Lycan. Maybe more so. Renard would be kicked out if anyone discovered them.

"She didn't tell you?" he asked in confusion.

"Besides her bringing me the bird, Arthur won't let me see her. I'm surprised he even let me see you." He was such a complete turd.

"Othello approved us to be turned so we didn't have to wait for the next group. We went in together, Lisbeth. He's one of the turned now."

"You're kidding me! Like seriously messing with me.

Right?" Cameron shook his head and I sat down on the closest armchair to process the news, which while it was a good thing, all things considered, it was still a surprise. "How'd Olivier take it?"

Cameron leaned against the couch back. "At first she was furious. He didn't tell her, so she found out afterward. I've never seen her so angry. I mean, she's loved him this whole time, but she wanted him to have a real family, something he can't have with her. Like what you wanted for me. But she needed him. Even without her saying so, he knew she wouldn't make it without him, not after what's happening with you. So he bit the bullet and did it."

I hated the thought of Cameron and Renard locked in the coffins. I was glad I hadn't been there to hear Cameron scream. It would've destroyed any bit of sanity I'd managed to scrounge up for this visit.

He saw my face and knew what I was thinking about. "I thought knowing what I knew, and hearing the screams every year would prepare me, but..." He shook his head slightly, trying to shake the memory off. "It didn't." He took a heavy breath and stared at the ceiling. "So," he said to divert the conversation. "How are you? I mean besides being locked up in here for months. Olivier says you had a boyfriend?"

Had Knight been my boyfriend? I pressed my mouth together and fiddled with the hem of my dress. "Yeah, kind of. I met a werewolf."

Cameron looked shocked, but he was grinning from ear to ear. "You hooked up with a werewolf? You bad girl, you. What a rebel." I rolled my eyes and almost smiled. "What happened with him?"

"He umm..." The lace on my dress hem strained from me pulling on it. "They took him away. To be executed." Cameron stilled and waited for me to say more. "I miss him. Every day. But he's... he's gone. They won't let him live. I know they won't." It was silent as I tried not to let the tears come out.

"I'm sorry, sis," Cameron said after a few minutes.

I gave him a little smile. "You never called me sister before. I'll have to get used to that."

He smiled back. "Go ahead. I've got time."

Just as I'd started to feel a tiny bit better, Arthur slammed the door open, ruining the moment. "Visit's over," he declared. Cameron hugged me tightly and left. As soon as he was gone, I smelled lilacs right behind me. I turned and buried my face in Balthazar's coat. If I held him close enough, I could pretend I was hugging someone else. The only person I wanted to hold in my arms.

"Where have you been?" I mumbled against his jacket.

"I'm sorry, my love. I got here as soon as I could."

I missed Knight so much. I missed Cameron already. I missed being outside of my room. I hated that Cameron had been turned, even if it was what he wanted. I couldn't take this anymore. Every part of me was numb, and I needed to feel alive again.

I looked up at Balthazar, tears running down my cheeks, and pleaded, "Make me forget." And I did something I had tried to never do, but once it had been done, I couldn't take it back.

I kissed him.

He was shocked at first, how could he not be, but he leaned into the kiss and caressed my cheeks with his large beautiful hands. Kissing him felt as amazing as I'd always pictured it would be. When he pulled away from me, he looked wary, but there was a flush on his face that was particularly pleasing. "What are you doing, pet?"

"I'm never going to see Knight again. The Council is debating my fate as we speak. It doesn't matter what I do anymore. I'm going to die soon, and you have never chastised me for anything in my life, so don't you dare start now. I'm dying inside, please, Balthazar."

Balthazar was clearly having an internal struggle over whether to have a moral complex about kissing me, but eventually, his instincts won out and he grabbed me for another soul searing kiss. "Oh, I've missed kissing," he breathed against my lips. I wondered how long it had been since he'd kissed someone.

Kissing him felt right, and wrong at the same time. Right because somehow being with him made sense. Wrong because I still longed for Knight, and I had no room for anyone else right now. Maybe ever. That hardly mattered, and I pushed all other thoughts away, because I was going to have my fill of Balthazar before this day was over.

Consequences be damned.

4

ASKING FOR MY OPINION

*K*night's scent enveloped me in my sleep, and it chased away all the grief and loneliness enough where I felt like I could breathe again. When I awoke the next morning, Balthazar was gone, with only the scent of lilacs on my pillow to remind me he'd been there.

Before that night, I'd been dead inside, but as I lay in bed letting everything wash over me, I felt anything but numb. One night with Balthazar had put part of me back together, which was exactly why I'd done it. It wouldn't last, but hopefully it would hold until my trial.

"Breakfast," Arthur called from the living room. Getting up, I put on a robe and stepped across my carpet to find Arthur standing in the open doorway already. A quick glance at the wall clock by the door told me he was off schedule, and he was never off schedule.

"It's not 8 am," I noted, taking the tray and the bag of blood. "You're two hours late."

"I figured you needed some rest after what I heard going on in here." *Oh my god.* He'd heard everything. My cheeks flushed, and I turned from him to put the food down onto one of my end tables.

"Trust you to not be a gentleman and leave your post to give me some privacy." I picked up the blood bag and made a hole to suck through, emptying it quickly.

"In hindsight, I'm sorry that I didn't."

"Pervert," I tossed behind me, along with the blood bag for him to catch. "Next time you listen in on me, I'll kick you so hard you'll lose feeling in your extremities."

"Noted," he responded, and left the room.

After that, Arthur kept the conversations at a minimum and never looked me in the eye. I was very happy about that because it took me over a week to stop flushing when he walked in. I didn't like him, do *not* mistake me, but now I felt exposed in front of him. Not a comforting image, being exposed in front of Arthur. How would he even respond? Curled lip, vacant eyes like everything else, or maybe it would crack him finally. Food for thought.

Days continued on in my tower prison like leaves falling from the trees. My sanity remained intact, but Balthazar did not return. Maybe I'd scared him off. Maybe I'd reminded him too much of the lady in my family that he loved once. Maybe I'd hurt him.

On day 158, according to Arthur, he brought me my food but remained in the doorway instead of leaving.

"I understand you're mad at me," he said after a few minutes of standing there like a creeper.

Oh, so now he was going to talk about it? "What, for eaves-dropping like a perv?" I stabbed the blood bag and started sipping it. Gods, it tasted awful. Was this a bad batch? Maybe the human had been sick.

He sighed. I'd been listening to his sighs long enough to know he was trying to not growl at me for annoying him. "Not that. Before, with the Lycans. I was trying to protect you." When I didn't turn around, he continued. "We crossed paths with the Lycans that were hunting the werewolf. They made it clear that if we didn't assist in their search for him, they'd kill you when he was brought in. There was no way to save him. I could only save you."

I turned from my tray, crossing my arms over my dress, the fabric rustling under my fingers. "You still lured him to the warehouse. That's why you were shouting in the woods like it was a church social."

"It was a territory threat, one of the few things he can understand when he's a wolf. I was trying to scare him away so he wouldn't follow us. I didn't realize he'd already thought of you as his mate and would've followed no matter what I did."

"You were trying to save him," I said quietly, finally under-standing, after all this time. Finished with the blood, I picked up a piece of toast from the tray to wash the nasty taste out of my mouth. "Why are you telling me this?"

He held out his hand and I stared at it like a beacon of hope. "Let's go."

Oh. Oh gods. I was going to cry.

"Don't tease me," I warned with a mouth full of toast, lifting a finger at him and shooting a death glare. "You tease me and we're done."

"Let's go," he repeated in that same flat tone. Eagerly, I jumped forward and he took my arm on a magical journey out of my rooms and down the hallway.

After so long! The sights! The sounds! Everything was new and beautiful, even though it all looked exactly the same as it had for decades. The same boring castle was magnificent.

As excited as I was, it was odd being in the rest of the castle after five months of suffocating confinement in the same damn rooms. I'd grown tired of the same colors and designs. At least if they exiled or killed me I wouldn't have to look at any of it anymore. I was hoping for killing me, because *god*, I couldn't take more of those same walls and same furniture and same everything.

Everyone we passed on the way to the bigger drawing-room gave me a look. They were clearly angry that I'd broken the second vampire law. I could tell a few of them knew about Knight because they looked less angry and more disgusted. Eww, it's the vampire who let a Lycan kiss her.

We turned the hall and I suddenly felt something coming up my throat. I gagged and held it down with a fist over my mouth. My stomach was in knots and flip flopped around like a dying fish.

"Let's go," Arthur said for a third time, tugging on me. I heaved again but didn't let it come out. "What's wrong?" He wasn't concerned, just annoyed.

"I'm not sure, I think the blood was bad." My stomach flopped again in a final protest and the churning faded to a low whisper. It was just nerves. My trial was finally here. Everything would be okay.

Satisfied I wasn't going to blow chunks everywhere, Arthur opened the door to the bigger drawing-room and shoved me slightly so I'd go in. Waiting for me there in the large, hunter green room was the head of every Order on the planet, twelve in total, Othello among them. They sat in a half circle behind a very official looking desk that hadn't been there before. It felt like model U.N. or the Evil League of Evil. They were definitely the Evil League of Evil.

"Nice desk. When'd you buy that?" I asked Othello. Arthur flicked me hard in the ear for talking, because being my jailer hadn't softened him towards me, apparently. Pain shot through my lobe and my stomach rolled again. "Oww! What is your problem?" I wanted to hit him back but I thought better of it. He'd probably hurt me again.

Othello gave Arthur a pointed glare. "Stop that, Arthur. She's not an unruly child." For once in my life, I was glad Othello was there. Maybe he'd order Arthur to leave his permanent residence at my door. Or at least let me go outside for five minutes.

A woman sitting near the middle of the huge desk stood up. With her salt and pepper hair, she looked much older than me, but I felt her age was only about five decades my senior. Peanuts in vampire years. "I am Castilla of the Order Acilino." She had a deep Spanish accent. "Elisabeth, you stand accused of disregarding your duty to slay any Lycan found within our borders. This is the second in our most sacred laws. To ignore it is punishable by death. Do you understand this?"

I took a deep breath and swallowed. "Yes."

"Normally these proceedings would be overseen by the head of the oldest Order, but as that Order is the one you belong to, Othello has not been allowed to supervise the hearing."

I glanced at him and he looked apologetic. No doubt he would have swayed the vote in my favor, which was why he'd been replaced. "I understand," I told her with a nod.

"We shall proceed," she said with finality.

"Wait." I knew that talking out of turn was absolutely inappropriate, and might earn me another ear flick from Arthur, but I couldn't help it. "If I may ask. Why was I locked in my room for five months? That's quite a long time to gather everyone together. Was there something else you had to do first? A soirée to attend?"

Castilla wasn't annoyed, which was good. I could see she had an ocean of patience, and respected me just enough for her to be kind instead of patronizing. "We've been here this entire time, Elisabeth."

Now I was the one annoyed. They had been in this castle

all this time? Oh that old bag upstairs unable to leave her room? She can wait a little longer, this wine won't drink itself, you know! I ground my teeth together and took as deep a breath as I could without making noise.

"Why wasn't I summoned here sooner, like say, when you first got here?" I couldn't help being snippy.

My tone caused a stir across the curved desk, but Castilla graciously let it slide. "The reason it has taken this long to summon you is that we were very divided on a detail of your case, a detail many have come forward about as advocates for you."

"And what would that detail be?" I asked her, curious to say the least.

"The Lycan you spared was a child and had not yet felt the change. Was he human? Was he Lycan?"

"You couldn't decide," I stated. It made sense. We had another rule about preserving human life as much as possible. No wonder they were so torn.

"This is a very serious offense," she emphasized, her dark red lips pursed making wrinkles on her face. "Some believe it doesn't matter. He will one day become a Lycan, so therefore, he is to be treated like one. Others believe he is human until he changes. Five months," she said wearily and ran a hand across her forehead, her many bracelets clinking against each other. "Five months and we still cannot come to an agreement."

"And yet you've summoned me."

"No matter what the offense, the accused can plead their

case. In some cases, it doesn't matter. Yours, it may. So. Proceed." She sat down and straightened her ivory jacket, her eyes fixed on me. All twelve of the heads waited for me to speak.

Where should I begin, I wondered. Might as well start with the basics. Standing up straight, I leveled the curved desk with my serious face.

"I spared a Lycan child," I confessed. "I knew he was within the borders, but I still did it."

"Why?" one of the heads asked.

"Because he was a child. Despite my faults, I don't kill children. It may not be a rule you enforce, but it's important to me." I hoped they would respect that. I wasn't holding my breath, though.

"But you knew he was a Lycan," another said.

I nodded. "Yes. I knew."

"And you did it anyway?"

The urge to roll my eyes was very strong. "Like I said. He was a child."

Castilla spoke next. "And after Arthur came, you ran."

"Yes."

"Why?" she asked me.

The answer had become clear to me over my imprisonment as I'd dealt with the guilt of Knight's involvement. It was still a paltry excuse.

"I'm old. Not quite as old as everyone here, but we're not very far apart in age. I didn't want my 400 years to go to waste." And my selfishness had ended a life. A life much more precious than my own. I looked down at the green carpet and felt another lurch inside my stomach. I hid it with a cough.

"Why run?" Castilla questioned. "You knew Arthur and the Hunters would find you eventually."

"I was scared. Everyone knows when the Hunters are involved it means someone is going to be executed. I didn't know you held trials. I thought you just killed first and didn't care if the judgment was fair or not."

"We haven't held a trial in a long time, since before you were born. I'm not surprised you thought this," Castilla said solemnly. "Understand, we hold the first law above all others. Don't kill other vampires. Every time we end a vampire life, it is a tragedy."

I felt deflated by her words. It had all been for nothing then. If I'd never met Knight, the other Lycans would've never found him. He'd still be alive. He was dead now because of me being a coward. Because I did something I thought was morally right, and then I ran instead of facing the consequences. And Knight paid the price. I'd never forgive myself for that. Never. A broken sob escaped my lips and I held down another heave.

Castilla took my tears for something else. "Calm down, please. I'm sorry that you were scared and thought you had to run. Luckily, that won't sway our decision. Running is not an offense."

Oh effing awesome. I wouldn't want to be executed for running. "Because Arthur always finds us?" I couldn't help sounding as annoyed as I felt.

She pursed her lips like I was pushing her patience. "Correct." She waited a bit for me to get my emotions under control. I focused on the hunter green walls around me and pushed Knight from my mind so I would stop crying. Mourn him later, when you're not on trial. "Do you have anything else to say?"

I sighed and looked down finally. "When I spared the boy, I wasn't sparing a Lycan. I was sparing a child. He didn't have their scent. He smelled human."

"And if he had smelled of wolf?" Castilla asked.

I looked straight into her dark grey eyes and spoke the truth in my heart, no matter the consequences.

"I don't kill children."

The heads dismissed me after that so they could debate on a technicality again. I hoped it wouldn't last another five months. Arthur took my arm and started leading me back to my rooms. My stomach was flopping over and over, I could hardly catch a breath.

"Tough crowd, amirite?" I joked, and put a fist to my mouth to hold it closed. My feet stumbled and I struggled to stay upright. Arthur's hand gripped my arm and dug in with a crushing intensity to keep me from falling. I was sure I'd have bruises later. "I don't feel so good, jailer. I think that blood was…"

Halfway up the stairs, amid dozens of stares from other

Born vampires, my stomach lurched and I threw up bagged blood and a toast all over Arthur's army boots.

Oops.

I waited for him to rip my head off, but he merely pulled me up by the arm so hard I wondered if he had dislocated it, and dragged me up the rest of the stairs, down the hallway, and deposited me inside my suite. My stomach was still upset and I had to run to the toilet to heave until there was nothing left to expel.

Olivier burst into my bathroom and saw me leaning over the expensive polished toilet. "What in the hell, Lisbeth? Did you drink some bad blood?"

I looked over at her in confusion. "I threw up two minutes ago, how are you already here?"

"This castle is tiny, everyone knows everything. Plus, I was in the lobby, so I saw it. Right on Arthur's shoes, too." She gave me a round of applause. I laughed and heaved again over the bowl. "Where's the blood you had today?"

"Living room," I got out before I had to gag. She walked over and brought it back with her, stuck a finger inside the plastic bag, and licked it. She smacked a few times and looked confused. "This blood is fine. Vampires don't throw up unless the blood is bad."

"It tasted bad when I drank it, I swe—" Heave.

And then a thought occurred to me as I sank my butt onto the tile floor and wiped at the sweat that had gathered on my forehead.

"Or unless..." I focused my power inward and searched my body.

There it was. The tiny sac inside my womb that couldn't be noticed yet without focus, and the result of my choice to sleep with Balthazar.

A baby. I was pregnant.

I mean, I knew Incubi were 100% fertile with human women, but I'd assumed they wouldn't be able to get a vampire pregnant. It seemed genetics hadn't cared who he'd tupped because I was having his baby.

I came back to myself and gave it all away with the look on my face.

Olivier stared at me in horror, the empty blood bag slipping from her hand and falling on the tile floor. "You... with who, Othello?"

"Oh *gross*. I'm not in the mood for jokes. If I have to think of Othello's O-face, I'm going to throw up again."

She wasn't laughing. "I'm serious. He's mated to Marie now. You cannot be pregnant with his child."

Well, that was new. And gross. "It's not Othello's, I promise." That was too horrible to imagine.

"Then whose? The werewolf?" She made a gagging noise and I glared at her.

"Sadly, we only kissed. Plus I'm sure biology wouldn't allow it." Would it though? If Knight had lived, could I have had his child? I clearly was able to mix my genes with another species.

"Then who?" Olivier asked again, her hands on her hips.

I couldn't say it. I'd see the way the Lycans had treated

Knight because he wasn't like them. If anyone knew I was carrying the child of an Incubus, I was sure they wouldn't let it live.

"I can't say who."

"Look. I know that Othello has always been nice to you-"

"It's not his child, god that is so disgusting! I would never!"

She pursed her lips and I could tell she didn't believe me. Great. My best friend thought I was getting busy with Creepzilla. "You should get rid of it. Right now. Before anyone finds out. I'll get you the stuff you need."

"No," I told her firmly. "I refuse. No." How could she even suggest something like that? Children were so rare for us, to get rid of one was like shooting a tiger. "I'm fine. You should go back to Renard," I spat out, making sure she knew exactly how pissed I was about both things.

Now she was the one to look guilty, and I ignored the slight twinge in my stomach at her sadness. "You know?"

"Cameron told me. Thanks for sharing."

She went to the sink and brought me a wet rag to wipe my face off as a peace offering. Folding her dress underneath her, she sat beside me on the cold tiles. "I'm sorry I didn't say anything. You lost... the werewolf. I didn't want to make you feel worse."

"You're happy, that's good." I smiled at her, sincerely pleased with her love life, even if mine was in pieces.

"Speaking of boys," she said, turning to me with her eyes narrowed. "You just lost someone you loved and you're getting pregnant with someone else?"

"Judgy much?" I stood up, my stomach appeased for the moment, and walked over to stare at myself in the mirror over the sink. "Knight is dead. He wouldn't want me to mourn him forever. It's not like I did it straight off. It's been months. Five of them." Feeling guilty was inevitable, no matter how much I'd enjoyed it, but now that there was a child in the mix, I didn't regret what I'd done, and I'd keep telling myself that until I believed it.

She got up from the floor and flushed the toilet for me. "You're right," she conceded gently. "I'm sorry. I didn't mean to upset you."

I caught the slightest whiff of lilacs and it soothed my stomach further. "I'll be fine. I need to rest." Olivier hugged me and left. Two seconds later, Balthazar appeared from Cameron's old room. His eyes went down to my belly.

"Mine?" he asked. I nodded. "I'm sorry, Lisbeth. I should've said no to you. I had no idea this could happen."

I shook my head, finding a smile. "You wouldn't have said no to me so don't pretend otherwise. I was dying inside and I didn't care. I took advantage of you."

He chuckled. "That's never happened to me before, and it still hasn't so don't feel bad." He walked closer and kissed my forehead. "I still love you. If you ever need me in that way again, I'm afraid I will have to decline. Not because I don't want you, as much as you reminded me of..." I raised my eyebrows, shocked that he was about to confess how he knew me. He bit down on his lip to stop himself from saying too much. "My point is..."

"Okay, A. One day you are going to finish that sentence." He rolled his eyes at me. "B. I understand, and I am content to still be friends with you." I smirked, he grinned, and we stepped closer until I leaned in to kiss him warmly on the cheek, hugging him tightly.

He hesitated, and then he pet my hair, the same way he always did. "I will always be here for you. I promise that."

I moved one hand to my stomach and leaned my head against his shoulder. "I can't tell anyone you're the father. They might try to take the baby. They'll be afraid of it."

He put his hand on mine, over our baby. "The child of a vampire and an Incubus. We have no idea what she'll be."

My eyebrows raised in a thunderous rage. "SHE?"

His face went still. "What? Did I say she?"

I turned on him, grabbing his tie in my hands to yank him forward. "Do you have some magical baby gender knowing power? Because you just spoiled a nine month mystery."

He tried to look innocent and bat at my hands. "Noo-o-o?"

"You are *so* dead!"

5

SURPRISE

*T*he cat was out of the bag.

With my public display of barfiness, everyone knew or suspected that I was pregnant. The popular theory was either I was having Othello's baby or Knight's. I would've preferred the latter, and caught myself sometimes wishing she was his. She'd come out with his dark tanned skin and black hair, and his beautiful brown eyes. Every time the image came to me, I wept alone in my room for the child I was certain I'd never have.

The next day, I sat in the castle hospital wing with Arthur, waiting to see the vampire baby doctor. As every second passed, what started as a nice moment was quickly becoming a guilt fest. What kind of love did I have for Knight if I got pregnant with someone else, not even a year after losing him? Yes, I was trying to move on, and I didn't regret that, but I'd jumped into it with someone else so fast. Wouldn't I expect Knight to mourn me longer than a few months? What if I was in a coma for two months and woke up to find him with some blonde tart? I'd be so upset he didn't wait longer. Not that me being in a coma was the same thing as him being executed, but still.

It was good that Knight was dead. He would never want me now.

Arthur was in the chair next to me, arms folded over his chest, staring at a painting across the room. I'd only needed to tell him I had to come here and he brought me, no questions asked. He sat next to me quietly without comment. Who knew I'd legitimately appreciate his company for once.

"Thanks," I said after we'd been sitting for a few minutes. Not like there were other patients here or anything. I was the only pregnant vampire at our Order. Maybe the doctor was finishing up a level of Pong.

"Funny, I think you said thanks in the direction of my face. You must be delirious."

I picked up a very old edition of Highlights magazine and whapped him on the head with it. "That's for clipping my ear at the hearing."

He grabbed a copy of Vogue that looked like it was from the 80's and flipped it against my forehead just lightly enough that I didn't feel pain. "That's for being an incorrigible butt face."

My mouth dropped and I twisted to stare at him. "I am not a butt face."

He tossed the magazine and missed the coffee table so it slid onto the carpet. "Maybe not. But that is something you would say to insult someone, is it not? My insult skills are... slim to none."

I settled back into my chair and put my feet onto the coffee table. "I'm curious why you would need to learn such things. Considering you suck at them."

"Before I came here, I was alone for many years. One hand." He held one palm outspread in front of him. Each knuckle had scar tissue, like the harsh scars on his face. He could've only gotten those fighting a vampire or a Lycan. If the one thing that can harm us is each other, we leave scars behind. "I only need one hand to count the number of times I spoke aloud between when Olivier left me and I arrived to hunt you." His hand fell back to his lap. When I'd first heard him speak on that first day we met, the raspiness of his voice made me wonder if he rarely spoke. Now I had my answer.

I folded and unfolded my hands around my stomach. "Why would you do that? Not speak for so long."

He shrugged and his shirt crinkled against the wall. "It's easier to sort out your thoughts when you're not prattling about useless things."

"Do I need to hit you with the Highlights magazine again?"

The nurse finally came into the waiting room, apparently she was playing Pong too, and called my name. I stood up and followed her to the examination room with Arthur on my tail. Walking through the open door, I sat down on the examination table, Arthur stood in a corner, and we waited for a few minutes before the doctor came in. He wasn't very old, only a century or so, and I didn't know him very well, as we'd never interacted before then for obvious reasons.

"Lisbeth," he said brightly, checking the chart I'd filled out as if he didn't know my name. Everyone knew my name even if I didn't know theirs. I was infamous now, the vampire that broke a law, ran away, and then got knocked up after smooching a werewolf. Try living that down. "So, there's a little one on the way, I see?" *No I'm here for a flu shot.* What a twit. "Now, I mean no offense, but I have to ask since you left it blank on the form. Who is the father?"

I gripped the edge of my shirt so tightly my knuckles turned white. "That's private." It almost ended as a question but I stopped myself just in time. The facade had to continue. Not even the doctor could know who the baby's father was. It was probably short sighted of me, considering the cross-species circumstances, but I stuck to it and gave him a determined look.

"You're not mated?" he continued, probing me like the Spanish Inquisition. Single mothers were extremely uncommon amongst Born vampires, so it wasn't unfounded for him to be curious. We tended to only bump uglies when there was a ring involved. Or bonding ceremony, since we didn't wear wedding rings. I shook my head as an answer and continued staring right at him so he'd back down. "Right."

He wrote a few things on my paper and walked up to me to lean in close. "It's not his, is it?" He casually motioned to

Arthur, trying to be discreet. Uh, what the hell? My look of utter confusion, and dare I say disgust, made him straighten and step away. Arthur was hot, don't get me wrong. But hard pass. "Alright then. No father. That's not a problem. Good. Good." I rolled my eyes as he tried to pretend it wasn't a big deal.

After instructing me to lie down on the examination table, the doctor rolled some equipment over to me. It looked weird, not like the typical ultrasound machines I'd seen on television. "Special vampire ultrasound machines," he explained when he saw my confusion. "We only have the best here."

One of the machines had an arm on it, like the kind used for x-rays, with a digital display screen on top. He rolled it closer to me until the arm was over my stomach. A flip of a switch and the machine turned on, covering my belly with light. There was a tiny display screen on the side near my face so I could see what the doctor was seeing on top of the arm.

A baby.

I'd felt it inside me, and now I could see it as clearly as a photograph. Little fingers, little toes. My little one. She twitched, her oddly shaped body moving around in her little sac, and she stuck a tiny finger into her newly formed mouth. I reached a hand out and ran my fingers over the display. Over my baby's image.

"She's so tiny," I said out loud. My hands clenched and unclenched against my shirt, and I wished I had someone's hand to hold besides my own. Knight's hand. Tears came, from the baby or from Knight's face in my mind, I didn't know which. Both.

"You're about nine weeks along," the doctor told me, and punched more buttons so the machine made clicking noises like a camera taking a picture. Then he flipped the switch again and the image of my baby went away. I wanted to protest, but he handed me some photos he'd just taken and printed of her. They weren't black and white, they were full color images like he'd reached inside me and snapped a picture. "Come back next week and we'll take more."

With that done, he showed us out of the hospital wing, leaving me alone with Arthur, who was still silent like something had shifted his mood.

"You disapprove?" I asked him, tapping the photos against my hand.

He shrugged. "It's not against the law to get pregnant."

"You and law breaking. I could torture someone in front of you and as long as it wasn't breaking the law, you wouldn't blink an eye at me."

The beginnings of a smirk flashed across his face before it disappeared. "I'll talk to Othello," he said, shifting the subject smoothly like always. "You'll need to feed from humans while you're expecting. Bagged blood will just make you throw up again. Let's go." He started walking down the hallway, expecting me to follow.

"Thank you."

"Don't thank me," he said blankly, and continued down the hall.

In all my 400+ years, there was a very small number of things that I had not experienced, and most of them were things that I wasn't interested in like bungee jumping or being launched into space. Pregnancy was as foreign to me as an alien species.

Knowing the mortal species we shared the planet with as I did, being pregnant was something human females looked forward to and were expected to do. Female vampires, not so much. We were not expected to have children, our culture simply wasn't designed the same way. If we chose to live out eternity without ever giving birth, that was our choice. Sure, having progeny was great, but there was more than one way we created life. We could either have a child of our own or turn humans in the turning ceremony.

I had sired more of the turned than I could count, and I had never kept in touch with a single one of them. I created them, I trained them, and I forgot about them. The child inside me wasn't someone I could just give birth to and send on its merry way. He or she (most likely she, thank you, Balthazar) would be with me for the rest of my existence, assuming I'd be destroyed before my child was. That was the preferred outcome.

And beyond that, I didn't know how to raise a child. I'd never had parents, I grew up as a ward of the Order. The Order didn't tuck me in to sleep at night, and they didn't teach me how to ride a bike, or whatever it is that humans viewed as parenting. Hell, I recalled times when I was a very small child and they let me play with knives like they were toys. There was a lesson in there somewhere about the Order sucking as a parent. Not like the knives could've hurt me, but still.

Being an orphan eliminated one thing humans worried about. Most humans had hesitations about being a parent because *their* parents were horrible at it. They thought that because their parents yelled at them, they'd become a parent that yells. And that's partly true because you learn from what you see.

I had never seen anyone be a parent.

With vampire children as rare as they were, in our Order one vampire was born about every ten years, and that was not an exact number. Sometimes the gap was much longer. So, with the number of babies in our population, and considering none of the Born I was close to had yet to become parents, I was in uncharted waters. Couple that with the fact that the child I was carrying was the spawn of an Incubus, I had more than enough reason to freak out.

All of this was running through my head after Arthur had left me in my rooms. He was always silent, but this silence felt different. Something in my face must've exposed the turmoil underneath because Arthur returned twenty minutes later with a tray of tea. He came in without knocking, as always, not caring that I could've been changing, and set the tray down on the coffee table in front of the sofa I was sitting on.

On it was ginger cookies, a bottle of bubbling water, and tea that smelled like peppermint.

Without speaking, he sat down next to me and carefully poured the tea into a teacup which he passed to me. He poured some for himself, took a sip, and picked up the saucer with cookies. I took some and he put it back on the coffee table.

Having tea with Arthur was a twist, but I sipped my tea, a peppermint vanilla blend, and felt it creep in like a soothing balm. I took a bite of the soft ginger snaps and relaxed against the sofa as the flavor soaked into my mouth.

"These are good," I said, trying not to moan out loud. "People usually add peppers to ginger snaps. I don't like that." I took another bite and grabbed more from the tray.

"I remember," he said simply. I recalled me telling him early on in my imprisonment that I hated peppers. He remembered it. I mean, he had a perfect memory just like all of us did, but having it didn't mean we always remembered things every second of every day. My spaciness was proof of that. Or maybe I was just a special kind of weird. Plus, not even a perfect memory can make you remember details about a specific person. You have to pay attention. Somehow, him thinking of my comfort made me smile, though I couldn't say why. I still managed to be snippy for sarcasm's sake.

"Wow. My captor cares. Color me silly."

He sipped his tea and ignored my comment. "You are scared to be pregnant."

I bit into a second cookie and studied the wall in front of

me. "Didn't know you were a mind reader." Someone needed to get a life. I.E. One that did not involve living outside my doorway and trying to sort out my feelings. No one paid him to be my therapist. Even if they had, I'd expect a refund.

Setting his teacup down, he leaned into the couch to relax, like this was his house or something. "Olivier is judging you, so I don't think you want to talk to her about this. We are not friends, yes, but I have experience in these matters." That floored me. Him, knowing about pregnancy? I'd have been less shocked if I'd discovered he liked macramé.

"You have experience with pregnant vampires?" I asked him in disbelief. It was emphasized with my mouth opened as wide as the Panama canal.

"I had an unbonded mate before Olivier joined the Hunters. She became with child, and I was there for her pregnancy. She was scared, like you, at first. She had also been an orphan and didn't know how to be a parent. I may not be the perfect person to help you, but I will if I can." He had displayed only the barest hint of emotion during his speech, leading me to wonder what the outcome of his mate's pregnancy had been. I had a feeling it wasn't good, since she wasn't here with him. He didn't seem like a 'wham bam thank you ma'am' type of guy.

"Did she have the baby?"

His face went blank again, but it was not hiding every expression that tried to come out. "No. She went blood crazy from not feeding enough and attacked humans. We had to kill her."

To say I was shocked was an understatement. I'd thought the Council had some amount of leniency, but apparently, I was wrong. Not to mention, Arthur was way more devoted to his job than I'd originally thought. To have killed his own pregnant mate just because the laws demanded it, ending her life and the life of his child before it could be born. That wasn't right or fair. I thought I knew him. I suppose I never had.

When he finally spoke, he took a loud breath to compose his face. "The pain of doing my duty was greater than the punishment for disobedience would have been."

My hands scratched against my legs though I wasn't itchy. "I take it you didn't bring me tea so we could have a heart to heart?"

He snorted, his version of laughing. "Absolutely not."

I poured us another cup of tea and dropped a sugar cube in mine. "Your momentary lapse of feelings aside, I'll ask you a question, and when you answer, pretend that I care about what you say." Being prickly towards him was such second nature, I almost felt bad considering the topic of conversation. His following silence was permission to ask. "Would you kill her again, if you could go back and re-do it?"

His scarred knuckles clenched and then relaxed against his jeans. "Every day I wish I hadn't done what I did."

"That's not an answer." I shouldn't have been let down, but I was.

"My idea of loyalty is repulsive, I know," he admitted while he tapped his boot against the coffee table leg. "My offer of help still stands. No one else at this Order can, or will, give you the same assistance."

"I don't need help from you." I felt a small twinge of remorse. Remorse over being mean to Arthur. What was wrong with me?

He stood and left without looking back at me again.

6

TECHNICALITIES

*N*ow I was on my own. No boyfriend, no baby daddy, no best friend, and the only person who was offering moral support was a man who had killed his unborn child out of principle, no matter how he felt about it now.

Yay.

The good news was Othello quickly approved the request for me to be assigned two human companions. I didn't get to choose them, and they wouldn't be staying in my rooms since I was still under house arrest. My new companions were both big and burly, towering over me with their height. I had no doubt who had chosen them as Arthur had zero taste and probably viewed the process like picking a sheep instead of a cat. We didn't choose the companions based on the fact that they had blood in their veins, there was a certain connection we looked for. You wouldn't want to get stuck with someone for ten years and be bored to death whenever they opened their mouth.

My morning companion was named Benjamin. He was Italian and spoke with an accent that would have made human women weak at the knees, but it barely registered on my radar. His plan after his tenure was to use his severance money to start a restaurant outside of Venice, which he would be able to afford with the amount of money he'd be getting. I loved restaurants as much as the next girl, but he made it sound as boring as potato farming. Not that potato farming was boring, but it wasn't painting the Sistine chapel, I'll tell you that.

My evening companion was named Alfred. He was African, and I only called him Alfred because he refused to tell me his name. He was very cold towards me, which I assumed was because he didn't want to fraternize with a prisoner. I could see him and Arthur being best friends. If Arthur had friends, that is.

Not surprisingly, both of my new companions were former military as their looks suggested, and were most likely under Arthur's command, so they put my prisoner status above my needs. They let me feed, and they left. I only knew so much about Benjamin because he liked to talk while I fed, which as I mentioned was boring as hell. Still, it was conversation. Though, if I tried to respond to anything Benjamin said, he would get up and leave whether or not I was finished.

Oh, the company I keep.

Cameron came to find me a few days after the news had circulated around the castle of my scandalous visit to the baby doctor. I was playing mahjongg on my floor and Arthur swung my front door open, shoved Cameron in, and closed it behind him before I could say anything.

It still jarred me to see Cameron as a vampire, but he looked genuinely happy. I couldn't stay upset with him if he was happy.

"Onee!" he said happily, grabbing me in a hug. "I heard you're expecting! That's so awesome, high five!" I high fived him and he joined me on the floor.

"Yeah, it's umm... unexpected. To say the least." I worried my hands in my lap and shuffled the mahjongg tiles around on the carpet. "I'm scared. A little."

"What, you? Scared? Pffft. Don't be stupid. You're gonna rock this. You'll be such a cool mom that everyone else will be like, ooo damn, I wish Lisbeth was MY mom!" Instead of making me laugh, I started crying. Hormones. Cameron instantly reached for me and stroked at my shoulders. "Woah, hey, I was just kidding. Being a cool mom sucks. You'll be as uncool as a pocket protector." He lost his funny edge and carefully pulled me into his arms.

I couldn't speak over the sobs coming from my mouth. Was it really hormones, or was it that everything was still in the balance? I'd attended my trial but I was still a prisoner. Maybe I'd give birth in my rooms and they'd take her away from me. I couldn't bear that. To lose her when I'd lost Knight too.

My sweet precious Knight. I killed you. I effing killed you.

"What's wrong, sweetheart? Can you tell me like you used to?"

Like I used to when he was human.

"I lost him," I breathed finally, my voice scratchy with tears and my chest heaving as I gasped in a breath. "I waited four hundred years to find him, and I lost him. And now I'm pregnant before he's cold in his grave. What kind of woman does that? He's dead because of me, and I'm knocked up like he never existed. I'll never escape what I've done." Guilt I hadn't realized I'd been feeling was starting to overwhelm me like emotional vomit. So much for acting like it didn't matter that I'd slept with someone else. It did. It did so much.

Despite my tirade of sobs, Cameron chuckled and kissed my hair. "Silly girl. You're not supposed to escape mistakes. You're supposed to learn from them." He rubbed my arm and sat there with me while I got my tears under control. "One time, when I was still a teenager, someone said something to me. I never forgot it. Know what it was?" I shook my head. "Everyone has regrets. It just depends on what kind. A decision you should have never made, or being denied the chance to say goodbye."

I'd said that to him.

"I had debts from my time on the street, and I didn't tell you about them," Cameron continued. "They caught up with me. My debtors had me broken and bloody in an alley, and you fought them off, you protected me. I felt like I didn't deserve your protection because I'd brought it on myself. It was my fault. And then you said that to me. You made me understand that everyone makes mistakes. No one is above them."

I smiled at the memory until it faded back to sadness. "But I moved on. I moved on from my soul mate. What does that make me?"

"It makes you..." He broke off, laughing to himself behind his hand.

I sat back to look at him. "What?"

Still laughing, he said, "I was going to say it makes you human." I couldn't help but laugh with him, and I felt some of the pain lessen, like loosening the stays of a corset.

We played with the mahjongg tiles, with me explaining how the game was played, and Cameron trying to build a tower with them instead of playing. Every so often he would glance over at his old room.

"Funny," he said once his tower was gaining height. "I keep thinking I can just go back to my room and take a nap or go grab something. It's a lot nicer than the basement."

"And you're better company than Arthur," I noted, putting another tile on his tower. Cameron smiled and picked up more tiles. "I'm still scared." He looked up from his work, concern putting a wrinkle on his pale forehead. "I've never been a parent before. I never had parents. I don't know what to do."

He elbowed me playfully. "I doubt that. I was so young

when I came to you, just 15, and you stood by me, Lisbeth. You were more my mom than my big sister. You raised me."

I hadn't thought of it like that, but he was right. I'd counseled him, given him boundaries, and made sure he stayed healthy. I loved him. That's what parenting was, right?

"Then you should be calling me *okaa-san*[1], mother," I said with a sarcastic smile.

Knocking the tower over, he grabbed my arm and whined in Japanese, "Okaa-san, buy me a popsicle!"

Not two weeks later, the Council called me back again.

Arthur came to get me, and with his hand firmly on my arm, we went down to the bigger drawing-room.

"Easy with the goods, darling," I said gruffly, trying to lighten the mood.

"You're quoting something, aren't you," he stated with annoyance.

"You are without a doubt the worst vampire I've ever heard of." I flashed him my best pirate grin, but he ignored me. Dude had probably never seen a movie. There was always time to rectify that. "If I'm put back in prison, we're having a movie night. I will book no refusals."

His eye twitched and he adjusted his hand on my arm until I squealed in pain. "No way in hell."

Batting at his hand with mine, I wiggled and tried to get away. "You're so mean! You're hurting me!" At that, he loosened his grip and inspected my arm to see fresh bruises the size of his hands. He'd injured me before, but his unnecessary treatment pissed me off.

I slapped him across the face.

"Ass." I turned on my heels and walked through the bigger drawing-room doors by myself. The Council sat at the spiffy new Council of Evil table, all business and no smiles. Cozy little bastards.

My pregnancy had begun to show. I was a bean pole, making the bump look bigger than it actually was. More than a few of the Council members stared at my belly with unmasked distain as we approached them. Othello ignored me completely. Lovely.

Castilla stood up when we'd reached the center of the large room. "Elisabeth. It is nice to see you again. I see you are with child. Congratulations." Her words were nice, but she had about as much excitement as someone picking out a tomato. A very boring obnoxious tomato.

"Thank you," I responded. Arthur stepped up beside me, hands in front of him in a formal stance. He was still close enough to grab me if I felt like killing anyone, or whatever he thought I was going to do. Wildcard Lisbeth, that's me.

"Elisabeth, you stand accused of disregarding your duty to slay any Lycan found within our borders." If my memory served correctly, which of course it did, she was using her exact wordage from last time. "This is the second in our most sacred laws. To ignore it is punishable by death. Do you understand this?" Yep, she was repeating herself. Broken record? Glitch in the matrix? Oh right, I was supposed to answer.

"Yes."

"We shall proceed." She sat down and straightened her jacket. I was having a complete déjà vu. Had I traveled back in time? No wait, Othello's shirt was different. "In our previous session, you mentioned something about the child's smell. Could you please repeat what you said?"

The hell. I thought back and repeated my words verbatim, since we were all about repeating everything. "He didn't have their scent. He smelled human."

She looked satisfied, confusing me further. "Your words were the turning point. You testified that the Lycan child still smelled of human. Therefore, no matter what he will become in the future, he is still considered a human, and is worthy of our protection." She stood up, starting a chain reaction of all the other Council members to join her. "As a result of your testimony, the Council has decided, after a vote of 8 for and 4 against, that you are absolved of all crimes and may go free."

OH MY EFFING GOD.

These pissant tyrants locked me up for months on a technicality? Did it also take them five months to pick a new type of coffee creamer? How long did it take to decide on new shoes? Was there a giant stick up their butts? Affirmative on the latter.

And hello, since they'd been so undecided, what was stopping them from taking this verdict back? Hey, so, sorry about that, lulz, we're totes going to execute you anyway because

Bill here decided to change his vote. Turns out he hates children as much as he hates showers.

Even though I'd tried hard to mask my anger, Castilla paused to study me. "You are not pleased."

Girl read me like a book. I faked a smile.

"No, I am absolutely pleased." Lie. "I'm just a little scared you might decide you made the wrong choice in five minutes and lock me up again."

"Our judgments are final. We never revisit a case that has been closed. You are free for the rest of your life. Unless," she added with a tiny hint of humor, "you decide to break the law again." Hahaha, what a kidder. You scamp.

The council stood staring at me for a minute, expecting me to do something. Thank them? Beg for forgiveness? Flip them off? One of them caught my eyes, and he nodded his head towards the door. Oh, right. They wanted me to leave. I thanked them and left the bigger drawing-room. Arthur was behind me when I stopped walking just outside the doors.

"I expected you to lead me out," I commented, watching him shut the doors so gently they didn't make a sound.

Turning, he almost shrugged. "You're not a prisoner anymore. I have lost the right to hold you in your suite and oversee your movements."

"No more arm grabbing?" He didn't answer, he just walked away. For the first time in almost six months, Arthur was not within ten feet of me. I pumped my fist in victory. "Yesssss!"

I heard him hiss from further down a different hallway, "Keep silent, you imbecile! The Council can hear you!"

"What? I can't hear you over the sound of FREEEEE-DOOOOM– OH CRAP!" I ran before a quickly approaching Arthur could catch me.

The first thing I wanted to do with my freedom was spend some time away from the castle. If I had to look at my vanilla colored walls for one more day, I was going to murder someone.

Sadly, despite the homicidal thoughts it incurred, I had to go back to my room to pack a bag. Sitting on my sofa was the duffel bag Olivier had given me when I ran away. How had it gotten here? I'd left it behind in the teal convertible when I went after Knight. Then I noticed a large sticker on one of the handles that said, 'EVIDENCE.' Of course.

The bag and its contents used to smell like Knight. I brought everything up to my nose, hoping to catch a whiff of him, but it had been meticulously cleaned. All my comfy earthy clothes were in it, and oddly enough, even though I was finally back to my designer wardrobe, I'd missed my old clothes. Maybe they suited the new me better. I found a small bag in my closet and filled it with the clothes from the duffel. My bird was singing to me as I worked, and when I was finished packing, I picked her cage up carefully and brought her with me. We trekked down the stairs, past a group of judgmental eyes, and to the parking garage where I buckled her into Excalibur's passenger seat.

I was finally free. I just wanted to drive, and keep driving until I saw... something. I wasn't sure what I wanted to see. Maybe I needed a trip around the world. A few months here, a few months there. Except I was pregnant, and that meant I was chained to my companions. I couldn't leave town without them, and I had a feeling they weren't going to say yes to a month in Bali. If I had my way, I'd just get new companions, the type that would obey me, but contracts, and legal things, and blah blah blah. I was stuck with Benjamin and Alfred until I gave birth. Then I could choose a new companion. Someone fun. Maybe an artist. We could paint together in my sunny living room and make smores over vanilla candles. Maybe we'd paint the walls of my suite together and turn drab to fab.

My bird was chirping happily from her seat as we drove into town. I'd fed already and wouldn't need to again until dinner, leaving me with the entire day to myself. I passed by some town houses and I wished I could move into one and just live in town. Benjamin and Alfred could move in and we'd be far away from judgy vampires and stupid politics.

Who was I kidding? There was no way I'd be allowed to live in town. We lived away from humans for a reason, so we could live freely in our home. I couldn't exactly take Zumba classes without someone noticing there was something different about me. I just hated living in that stupid castle. Maybe someday they'd be different. Maybe someday I'd feel at home again. When one lives forever, anything is possible.

Shaking the thoughts from my head, I parked near the

center of town and took the birdcage with me. Nearby was the park I often walked in with Balthazar. I brought a hand to my small, round belly. A baby. My baby. Would she have dark hair like me? Balthazar's hair was the same color, so it was a safe guess. His eyes were blue, mine were purple. What would hers be? Would she be pale like me, or peach like him?

Or... would she even be normal. What would she grow into? She could end up being a monster. There were enough legends about Incubi being evil sadistic raping demons, even if Balthazar wasn't like that. Maybe he was just different than the others. Would my child be evil? I hated to wonder.

My bird started singing and I heard the same bird calls coming from the trees around me. She was talking to her own kind. I brought the cage up to my face and studied her little brown body. She'd gotten plump from the birdseed I was feeding her, and she stared back at me with a happy look. Should I just let her go? Maybe she'd be happier with her own kind. But then again, I'd had her since she was a hatchling. She couldn't survive on her own. The other birds around us kept calling to her, and she danced around her little cage in excitement. Maybe she needed a friend?

I found the nearest pet store on my phone, another item from the duffel, and started walking in the direction my phone led me. It beeped with a text from Cameron.

'Did you leave?' he texted.

'Just for a bit. I needed to walk.'

'Crap. I should've given you my phone. I need to hatch my eggs.'

'Eggs?'

'YOU ARE SO OLD.'

I chuckled as I put my phone back in my pocket. He was such a nerd. Eventually, virtual maps prevailed, and I stepped inside the pet store. It smelled like sawdust and birdseed, and was alive with the sounds of dozens of animals mixed with the hum and bubbles of tank filters.

"Welcome to the store," the owner said cheerfully from behind the counter. His skin smelled like lotion and kitty litter. He slicked his thin hair back and looked down at the birdcage in my hand. "Oh, look, you have a wild bird." He was almost reproachful, but wasn't about to toss me out and lose my business.

"She was abandoned. I have a license." Both were true. Not that I cared what a human thought of me.

The store owner relaxed and smiled a yellow stained grin. "Lovely! So, what can I help you with?"

I set my birdcage on the counter. "She needs a friend."

He then proceeded to list off perfect matches, and obviously he was suggesting the most expensive birds. He knew a high roller when he saw one. However, he made one crucial suggestion that I couldn't ignore.

"Her cage is too small," he added when he was finished showing me the birds he had. "Cardinals like to fly. She's not a baby anymore, she needs space."

I was back in the bathtub. I remembered the dolphins. Creatures that swam miles and miles of ocean reduced to a small pool. It seemed my bird knew my suffering. Longing to spread her wings but confined to a few feet of space.

My shoulders shuddered and I tucked hair behind my ear to chase the demons away.

The shop owner's top choice for a companion was a Lovebird. He had one that had never mated and would be more receptive to a new friend. It was a little purple and white bird, the same purple as my eyes. Removing it from the cage, he put it into a little cardboard box that had holes in it. "Are you sure I can't interest you in a larger cage?" he asked slyly as he was ringing up the Lovebird. All the cages he had were metal and boring. His sales pitch would go nowhere.

"No, thank you. I'm an antique kind of girl." I paid him and left with my two birds. We went back to the park and I sat down on a bench to do a quick search with my phone. I found some industrial looking aviaries like the pet store stocked, but eventually decided to commission a custom cage. I threw the idea and a large amount of money at the best designer I could find with the note, 'Impress me.' I probably made his day.

The thought of something new in my rooms gave me an idea. Maybe I didn't need an unrealistic dream of traveling the world. I was pregnant now, so I'd be given a bigger suite. One I could make my own and maybe help erase my unease. I quickly texted Othello's secretary/wife Marie and received a reply within a few minutes.

'You've been assigned new rooms on the top floor. You can begin moving as soon as you return to the Order.'

Things were looking up. Finally.

7

SETTLING A CRUSH

*E*ven with the excitement of new rooms hanging over me, I still spent several hours shopping in town. I'd hired an Uber just to drive my birds back home so I didn't have to worry about them. I instructed the driver to deliver them to Cameron, and texted him to put my new bird in with the cardinal so it wouldn't be stuck in the box.

Olivier was waiting in the foyer when I returned, holding my birdcage and glaring at me. "You sent an Uber." I didn't answer so she continued. "For birds."

I shrugged with a smile. "I couldn't take them into the store. What would you have done?" I was carrying a few shopping bags, but I managed to take the cage from her with my free hand and checked on the birds. They were sitting on the little perch chirping to each other.

"I would've just opened the cage door and let nature do its thing." She furiously wiped the hand that had held the cage on her leather dress like the birds had given her cooties.

"Pet hater," I threw over my shoulder as I started walking up the staircase. Othello's secretary had given me my new room assignment via text, so I headed up to the top floor, which was reserved for visiting guests, like the Council, and the oldest vampires. I had the seniority to live up there with the big boys, but I'd preferred my old room on the third floor. Until now, that is.

I eventually found my new room after passing several groups of Council members sitting in the top floor lounge. I had a feeling the ones glaring at me were some of the 4 people that wanted me to die. Nice talk, gentlemen.

The key was already in the door to my new suite, so I turned it and stepped inside. Completely bare of color and furniture, it had a similar layout to my old rooms with a corner window spread, but it was larger, with five bedrooms instead of two. One for the couple, one for the child, and three for their companions.

I sat down on the floor, set the birdcage and my bags down next to me, and hugged my knees to my chest. I felt tiny in the huge space. It was meant for a family. I was alone. My birds were still singing to each other. I looked over at them and saw they were already getting along.

My birds had more friends than me.

Olivier interrupted what was turning out to be a lovely decorating plan by bursting into my new rooms without knocking. I'd carried my desk and chair up from my old rooms and was sitting at it, pen and paper on one side and the birdcage on the other.

"Where's the fire?" I asked her. I was joking, but she looked way too serious. "Ummm, did you tear someone's arm off again?"

"You jest, but I am about to tear something in half downstairs, and it won't be pretty if I do."

I got up and walked to her calmly. "Okay, what's wrong?"

"It's the turned. You know I've been teaching them on my own, and that's been a damn parade." She made a raspberry sound with her tongue in frustration. "I am capable and smart, but I'm not you. I need you back. Get your job back. Please. I am begging you. The Princess of Morocco is begging you." I hadn't forgotten she was actually a princess, I just never remembered it when I thought of her. The fact that she was mentioning it showed how serious she was about this. And probably how serious she was about tearing something in half.

"Alright alright, calm down. I'll try to get my job back."

Olivier grabbed my hand and kissed it, then held it to her brown forehead. "Thankyou–thankyou–thankyou..."

I patted the top of her short curly black hair. "There there. Now, what's going on with them that's so aggravating?"

She straightened and growled, "Everything!" She paced the

floor. "They don't listen to me anymore. At every turn, it's 'Why can't we do this?' and 'That's a stupid rule!' and 'You can't tell us what to do!' It's a *nightmare*! Plus, Renard is with them so he gets to see me yelling at them just to keep them in line!"

"Yelling isn't the preferred method," I pointed out.

"I'm not you," she repeated. "I don't solve things with words and explanations. I solve them with a gun in their face."

"Please tell me you haven't tried that."

She angrily crossed her arms over her chest. "Othello said I couldn't have a gun." I raised my eyes to the heavens in thanks. "I feel powerless. When I was out as a Hunter, I knew what was expected of me, how I was supposed to react, and how things would play out. The turned are wild cards. Especially this group."

"I hear and acknowledge your words. I will go see Othello right now to get my job back." I went back to my desk to put my shoes on.

Olivier waved a hand at me. "I can go for you." She sounded like she was just trying to be helpful, but she had a look on her face that didn't speak helpful. I narrowed my eyes at her.

"He's not the father, I can see him whenever I want to." She put her hands up in an 'if you say so' shrug because she still didn't believe me. I rolled my eyes and left, pushing her out the door with me.

"Hello, Marie," I greeted cordially when I'd reached the side corridor outside of Othello's office. In the Born part of the castle, the carpet was hunter green and the walls a creamy beige, in keeping with our hunting lodge theme of décor. All we needed was some mounted deer heads and we'd look exactly like a British smoke club.

After standing for several minutes, wrinkling my nose at the painting of fox hounds taking down a stag that was hanging behind Marie's desk, I realized she was full-on ignoring me. Now that she was Othello's mate, it seemed she still hadn't learned to not hate me for grabbing his attention.

I lifted my fist over her walnut desk, right where she had an antique glass lamp. I could break it easily. "If you're too busy to talk to me, I can always put a hole in your desk."

Marie bounced up, getting between my fist and her antiques. "Othello is *absolutely* busy. I'm sorry, but he can't see you right now."

Instead of punching her in the face, which would have made me very happy, I crossed the short distance to a couch on the other side of the hallway and planted myself on it. Marie buried her face in a blue folder, still ignoring me, and as I rolled my eyes, I picked up one of the mints Marie kept on a lamp table beside the couch. It tasted like soap. Why would she have soap that looks like candy?

Sitting there, it worried me that the turned were acting unfavorably. Even though they usually questioned our methods and rules, they usually were okay with our answers.

Though I hated to do so, I slightly suspected Olivier was blowing it all out of proportion with her short temper. It was easy to blame an unruly child's behavior on the child itself, and not on the person in charge of them. Still, I was open to both sides of the situation.

Othello came from his office just then with Castilla, of all people. They shook hands and said a few business pleasantries before they noticed me. I tossed the mint wrapper into the bin next to the sofa and stood up with a smile.

"Elisabeth," Castilla said with a respectful nod. "We were just making arrangements for the Council members to be sent home. Your castle is extraordinary, but I can't say I'm not excited to see Spain again." They'd been here so long, but that was their own fault for being indecisive.

"I'm sorry everyone had to stay here for such an extended time," I apologized, feeling no guilt whatsoever. Now that I wasn't under trial, Castilla had much more warmth to her, and she smiled at me like we were friends. So not.

"You should be honored we were here for so long. We have a profound respect for you. There are very few of us that are as old as you. It would have been an utter tragedy to end your life, and I'm very glad it did not come to that." She stepped over to me and kissed me on both cheeks. "May I?" she asked. I didn't know what she meant until she gestured to my belly. I nodded, and she placed a hand on my stomach before closing her eyes. "Mmm, a sweet child. She will be strong, like her mother." She. More spoilers. Castilla stopped smiling and concentrated on what she was sensing. "She's different. I can't tell what I'm seeing." I lifted Castilla's hand from my stomach. I didn't want her delving too much. I should have never let her do that. She straightened and tried to smile. "I'm sorry, I must be tired. I'm known for baby reading. I can tell things about children when they're still in their mother's womb. That was... strange." My hands automatically went around my stomach, as if I was trying to protect my child from her. She shook her head and smiled wider to hide her unrest. "Ignore me, I'm an old soul. I saw love. This baby will bring you much happiness."

I thanked her and she left, thank god.

Othello smiled when I turned to him. "Lisbeth. What can I do for you?"

"I need to discuss a few things."

He held out a hand towards the open doors. "Come. We'll talk in my office." Marie tried to follow us with an entitled smirk, but Othello shut the door in her face. He sighed heavily and went to sit behind his massive dark brown desk. "You're wondering why I chose her," he said. Actually, I didn't care. He was free to do whatever he wanted. "She's annoying, I won't lie. But I needed a mate. I thought if I was mated, they might let me oversee your trial. It didn't work." As usual, he made a pointless gesture for me and didn't think of himself first. Gods, this man was hopeless.

"Now you're stuck with her forever," I said. He looked unhappy, and I felt slight guilt over it. Slight.

He shook it off like it meant nothing to him. And she probably didn't. "So. What did you need from me?"

"I'd like my old job back, if that's acceptable. Olivier needs my help with the turned."

"Done. Anything else?"

"Just like that?" I asked in surprise.

"Just like that," he answered back.

"You do remember I was on trial, right?"

"And you were pardoned. There's no reason to keep you from doing anything." He stood up and retrieved some paperwork from a file cabinet, bringing them over for me to sign. "The papers for getting your job back." I signed them with his big feather pen and handed the stack back, then he took it to his desk and put his seal on them. "I'm sure you've been informed that the turned have been a bit... unruly as of late." That's what he calls it? "I expect you and Olivier to report any changes to me. It's your job to control the turned. Find out what's going on down there, and end it." I nodded and waited for him to dismiss me. Instead, he came out from behind the desk and stood in front of me. He had his serious face on. Was he going to hit on me? "People think your child is mine. That's why Marie is acting like that. Not that she was much better before. I assume you know of this rumor?" I wasn't surprised he was bringing this up, but it made me uncomfortable. At least he wasn't flirting with me like usual.

"Olivier mentioned it."

He studied me, maybe waiting for me to confess who the father was, maybe feeling hurt that I'd found someone else that wasn't him. Owing to his very long and extended crush on me, I wasn't expecting what he said next.

"I apologize for the affection I showed you before. I knew it was unwanted, and I pushed it on you without consideration for your feelings. Being with Marie has certainly shown me what that feels like."

I saw a glimpse of the regret I assumed he didn't have over choosing Marie. A minuscule part of me felt bad that I'd been slightly mean to him over his affection towards me. I tried to smooth it over by smiling at him. "You were fond of me. It's not your fault."

He shook his head, tapping his long, yellow fingernails against the wood of his desk. "I was fond of the *idea* of you. When you left as a fledgling, you had a taste of the world. You came back different so I was certain you wouldn't stay. It scared me, and I thought that if I could make you love me, you'd never leave again. And then it just became a habit, showering you with gifts and my attention. I had done it for so long I forgot why I'd started. I forgot that you were once somewhat my daughter." While it all made sense, he was, as always, misguided in his actions.

"I never loved you as a father," I told him blankly, feeling slightly bad about it. A look of hurt flitted across his face, but then it was gone. "Maybe now we can be friends?"

He reached out for me and I stepped into a hug. I expected to feel the revulsion I usually felt when I was this close to him, but that sensation didn't come. Instead, I felt relief. Extreme, relaxing relief.

"I'm sorry," he said as he rubbed my shoulder. "We wasted so many years. I wasn't there for you when you needed me, and I alienated you from the rest of the Order. You were never fully invested in any part of our world except for your job. You're my right hand. You should know everything that goes on here, but you stayed away. I neglected my duties to you." He let me go and took a step back to give me space. "Please, let me make amends for all that I've done."

I'd never expected such a turnaround from him. He was right, I'd kept my distance from everything in the Order that I wasn't part of. I didn't educate myself about anything I didn't need to, because it would've meant being near Othello. Maybe if I had, I'd have known how to deal with James, and I would have known the Council gives fair trials. I wouldn't have run. And I wouldn't have met Knight. I supposed it was better this way. It seemed everything had happened for a reason, even Othello crushing on me.

"We can't change the past," I told Othello, and managed a smile. "But we can make a new future. I'll be involved. You tell me what to learn or do, and I'll do my best."

"Splendid," Othello said with an answering, but appropriate, grin. "With regards to your child, I can tell everyone I'm not the father. I'll make a public statement."

"No. Please don't do that," I pleaded in a rush, almost reaching out for his hands. He raised his eyebrows in question, and I felt stupid reacting so strongly. "If they know it's not you, they might try to find out who the real father is." I couldn't take a risk like that. Castilla's baby reading had spooked me.

"Very well. I won't try to discover your motives. You'd tell me if there was a problem." He started walking to the doors and motioned for me to follow. "Get lots of rest, don't overdo it. I'll let you know when I need you." He opened the door and waved me out.

8

MANAGING THE HUNTERS

On the trek back to my rooms, I felt nostalgia over the past year and everything that had transpired along the way.

Breaking the law. Meeting Knight. Being bitten and forced into borderline servitude. Working together with the man who should've been my enemy to break free.

Then I'd fallen in love, for real, after centuries of waiting for the right person to come along. And just as quickly, he'd been taken away from me.

I'd been put on trial for my crimes while at the same time becoming pregnant. After months of will they won't they, I was set free, only to discover that not only had my best friend turned himself into a vampire, my baby daddy had deserted me.

The cherry on top was Othello finally leaving me alone so

I was free to continue whatever type of life I could have after all those things.

It would be a fresh start for me. I'd never truly felt part of the group. My closest friend was an outsider, so it only made sense that I'd secretly felt the same. Maybe it was not knowing who my parents were. Something had held me back. And now I could feel myself opening up again, because this was a new day for me. No more hiding in my room. I did that far too often, my imprisonment aside. It was time to change, from a recluse to... whatever the opposite of that was. Social butterfly? No. That sounded exhausting.

I returned to my rooms to find Benjamin and Alfred sitting on the floor playing cards. Without Arthur to instruct them, they were now under my supervision. They stood up when they saw me, and stood at attention. I was going to shoot Arthur for sticking me with them. I felt like someone else had picked out a cat for me, and the cat hated me.

"Gentlemen," I acknowledged, nodding. "You." I motioned toward Alfred. "I'd like your real name, please."

"You cannot pronounce it," he said in his thick African accent.

"Son, I'm over four hundred years old. I think I can keep up." He ignored me so I sighed in defeat. "Fine. Your name is Alfred now. You good with that?" He looked like he'd rather stick his head in the toilet, but he nodded. "Two of the bedrooms are for you. You can fight over who gets which one. It doesn't matter to me, so feel free. Where were you sleeping before now?"

"Arthur's room," Benjamin answered.

I noticed two army bags against the wall. Their only possessions, no doubt. I went over to my purse and fished out one of my credit cards. "Here. You can use this to buy furniture, or clothes, or a Monet painting. Hell, get yourself a statue of Aphrodite. Whatever you need. It has no limit." Benjamin took it and stared at the little card like it was the holy grail. They both looked at me with wonder and surprise.

"May we keep whatever we buy? When we are set free, I mean," Alfred asked cautiously. *Set free*, he said, like this was a prison. God, Arthur sucked.

"Yes, don't be silly. You can keep everything. I won't be needing it. So, you know, go crazy." The room was silent, except for the occasional chirps from my birds. It seemed the men hadn't been told that shopping privileges were part of the companion arrangement. I wasn't too surprised since Arthur didn't know our standards, or more like didn't care to know them. "Look," I told the two men. "I'm supposed to make you comfortable and happy while you provide me with the blood I need. That's how this works. So please, for me, go buy the things you need. They'll give you a car in the garage, and the stores in town know our address if they have to deliver anything." Benjamin walked to the front door, but Alfred stopped in front of me.

"Thank you, ma'am," he said, a genuine amount of respect on his face. Bet he felt bad for not telling me his name now!

I smiled back at my reluctant cats. "Have fun. But be back here later. I need you to help me assemble my bed when it's delivered. Don't forget to buy yourselves beds as well. You can't sleep on the floor."

"Arthur didn't care where we slept," Alfred said quietly.

Putting my reaction into words was an impossibility. With a sharp intake of breath, I held it together for their benefit. "I'm not Arthur."

Waiting until they'd closed the door behind them, I slowly closed my eyes and curled my hands to fists at my sides. That *bastard* had made a human sleep on the *floor.* There was no curse word, no insult, no nothing worse than that offense, short of killing a human without just cause.

I was probably having a hormonal mood swing when I stomped a death march out of my rooms, but I didn't care. I rode that mood swing down the stairs, through a hallway, and out to the backyard. Arthur was on the veranda, sitting at one of the café tables, sipping some very strong coffee like a butt-hole. Without ceremony, I slammed my fist down on the table in a rage, breaking it in half. Coffee splattered over his dark grey t-shirt and he scrambled to avoid it.

"What is *wrong* with you?" he demanded angrily. I was probably crazy to provoke him, but at the moment I didn't care. I was too pissed off.

We'd drawn the attention of everyone else on the patio. Olivier was suddenly beside me, and she grabbed my arm, probably trying to make sure I wasn't about to strangle Arthur, and she was right to fear my wrath. I pulled free from her hands and glared at the subject of my anger.

"I don't know what you were thinking when you took leadership of my companions, but you clearly have no idea of the protocols involved with that." A slight twinge came to my belly and I took a deep breath to cool off. "You have offended several of the rules we practice here."

"I haven't broken any laws," he huffed, crossing his arms over his broad chest.

"You made my companions sleep on the floor," I spat venomously.

Othello had arrived to hear my accusation, and instantly turned on Arthur with surprise. "Is this true, Arthur?" he demanded.

Arthur, for the life of him, had no guilt in his face. "They're army men. They can take it. I saw nothing wrong with it. My priority was–"

"Your priority was *caring for them*!" Othello's voice was reaching my level of anger. We had become a united front at last. "The humans we house here are never treated with such disrespect. I will give no allowances because of your status as a Hunter, and if this is the level of treatment you and the other Hunters give humans, then you are not fit to be in charge of them."

I could see when Arthur finally soaked in the gravity of what he'd done, even if he thought it was stupid. He turned to me and said, "I apologize for what I did. How can I make it right?"

Othello was the one that answered, because I couldn't find my voice. "All of you are suspended. You and the rest of the Hunters will remain here and be instructed in social protocols by Lisbeth and Olivier. And if I ever get a whiff of this behavior from you or from any of the other Hunters again, you will be stripped of your status as their leader." Arthur nodded humbly and left the patio as the gathered group dispersed, like a dog with his tail between his legs.

Still beside me, Olivier gently touched my arm. "You okay?" I nodded to her. I'd been so angry that my fangs had almost come down. I took a deep breath to calm myself.

Othello angrily pulled on the edge of his jacket and smoothed down his greasy black hair, turning to me. "I apologize, Lisbeth. When I gave him custody of your companions, I assumed he knew what that entailed," he said. It was nice to have him on my side again. "Are your companions alright now?" He said it so gently, like we were discussing babies instead of grown men.

"I sent them shopping for furniture and such. They didn't know that was allowed."

Othello sighed with a weary glance to the heavens. "What is this world coming to..." he muttered. "You're fine with instructing the Hunters?"

"I'll do my best. As in, I'll try not to strangle Arthur. No promises." He smirked and went back inside the castle.

Olivier waited until we were alone to comment. "You have no idea what you're in for. You can't handle Hunters. They're a different class of vampire."

"This is my world, Olivier. I can do anything."

I'd like to say my confidence had been well placed, but it wasn't. However, I was determined, and that almost made up for it.

The Hunters were less than pleased at their new arrangement. We assigned them new rooms because they'd all been bunking it without permission in the smaller drawing-room. They thought living in actual rooms was too stuffy. Embrace the stuffy, people. Embrace it.

By the time the Hunters had gotten settled and agreed to a schedule for their lessons, a week had gone by and they were antsy to get this over with. That didn't bode well for me.

Hunter class was being held in the smaller drawing-room, since they clearly all knew where it was. Twenty-nine Hunters had been on the chase when I was the target, but that was every Hunter from all over the globe. The number in America was smaller. Eight Hunters sat in the smaller drawing-room, lounging on chairs, sitting on top of things you're not supposed to sit on, and they all looked at me like they wanted my head to spontaneously combust.

It took ten minutes to get them to stop talking. I got their attention by threatening to revoke their feeding privileges, which as Hunters meant they could feed discreetly amongst the populous. Yeah, that's right. Lisbeth doesn't play around.

"Lesson number one," I started. I was instantly hit with a loud "Boooo!" from one of the girls in the back. She was sitting on a low bookshelf that was not meant for someone's rear end, and had her arms crossed over her chest. I threw a pen at her. To clarify, I threw it so hard it sunk into the wall next to her head like a spear. "I am not here to play games with any of you," I informed them frostily. "I am here to instruct you in proper respect for humans."

"Right, because Arthur made your 'companions' sleep on the floor. Big deal," one of them said, making air quotes at the word 'companions.'

"You don't understand what I'm trying to teach you. I get that. Think of it this way, you all have a respect for the law, right?" I waited for nods or a yes, anything. They remained silent. "Try and think of that respect for the law but make it respect for humans. Would you pass on catching someone because you didn't feel like it? No. Because you respect the law. And we don't make humans sleep on the floor because we respect them. They keep us alive. They give us years of their lives in exchange for their blood. Without them, we'd literally starve. There is a level of esteem held for all humans that live here. They're not pets. They're not food." I could see my words weren't working. How could I explain it in a way they'd understand? "Think of them like... your favorite weapon. That weapon keeps you alive, right? You'd never leave it dirty or drop it wherever. You clean it. You keep it close by. You make sure it has what it needs to keep saving your life. Gun. Human."

And magically, I saw a hint of understanding light up in their eyes. Right before someone shot a spitball at me.

I went to my doctor appointments alone now. Every time I saw my daughter on the tiny digital screen, my heart leaped. She was perfection. I'd amassed a collection of ultrasound pictures, all as realistic as regular photographs. I put them in a photo album I kept in my room.

My old suite had been very vintage. All yellows and golden tones, with furniture over a century old, and more than a few much older than that. They were all priceless pieces, from my Ming vase to my designer clothes. I gave almost all of it away. I had no interest in that life anymore. I wasn't the Lisbeth that liked and treasured those things. I'd treasured my possessions more than I'd treasured the people I loved. It was a common vampire mentality, but I didn't want to be like that anymore.

The only things I kept were my favorite books, the clothes I'd bought when I was with Knight, a few trinkets from my past, and of course, my birds. The trinkets weren't worth anything. One was a crudely carved wooden horse rattle Balthazar had made me when I was very little. All of the edges had been smoothed out from centuries of holding it and remembering the past. The other trinkets were similar, just trivial things people had given me like a necklace or a piece of ribbon. I treasured those things, but in a different way than I'd treasured everything else. I treasured the memories, not the objects.

My new room was larger, but like the living room, it had an almost identical floor plan to my old rooms. The wall of built-in shelves in my bedroom was mostly empty, except for one shelf of books and the trinket box. My closet held a small number of clothes and a few pairs of shoes. Everything in my suite felt too big, or I felt too small.

I hadn't yet decorated the rest of my suite, beyond my new birdcage. Apparently, when you throw a large amount of money at someone, they build things twice as fast. The cage was enormous, large enough for me to walk into without stooping my head. It was made out of sturdy wood that had been stained to a deep walnut color. The design made it look like a castle, with towers and little windows with glass. It was a bird palace, and I loved it.

My birds loved it too, as much as they loved each other. They'd grown very close over the two weeks since I'd bought the purple and white lovebird. As soon as I put them in the castle and shut the door, they fluttered and flew around, singing to each other a song of joy.

Benjamin came out of his room when he heard the birds happily chirping up a storm. "Ah, they are very happy now," he said with a smile.

They explored their cage and we watched them for several minutes. Eventually, they calmed down and sat together on one of the perches. They finally had room to be free, but they still chose to sit on the same branch. Just to be near each other.

My heart hurt looking at them.

"What are their names?" Benjamin asked, bringing me out of my momentary sorrow.

"I don't know. I never named them." I didn't know why I

hadn't done so. I wasn't big on having pets. I guess I didn't think it was necessary to name them.

Benjamin clicked his tongue at me reproachfully. "They must have names. It gives them a soul."

"Well..." I looked at them and cycled through names I'd always loved. "The lovebird can be Kanoa. It means one who is free. And the cardinal..." I watched her flutter and smile. "Blythe. It means filled with happiness."

"*Perfezione*. Perfection. It fits them."

We sat there on the floor for hours, just watching the birds enjoy their freedom, without talking to each other. It was nice. Just relaxing together.

Alfred came out of his room when it was time to feed, breaking the spell. Benjamin got up and left the suite to eat while I fed from Alfred, who then disappeared into his room again.

I had six more months with them. Maybe things would start to change.

In addition to instructing the Hunters in human etiquette, I was also training the turned. The group I'd helped with before running away had completed their training and were already gone. This group was new to me.

Normally I dressed very stylishly while keeping a business aspect to my appearance. I entered the bigger drawing-room wearing a white button-down shirt and dark brown cargo pants with my long curly hair pulled back in a very thick braid. Olivier was wearing a long black dress that was much more modern than her usual style. It suited her.

She looked up when I came in and looked me over. "Don't you look different. I like it," she said with a smile.

"You look different too. No more mermaid dresses? I'm curious to know why you gave up a life of sarcasm." She usually dressed like she was making fun of vampire stereotypes. As an answer, she rolled her shoulders up and down in a cute shrug. "Ah, so it was reviews from a certain gentleman?" I nudged her jokingly.

"Renard can keep his opinions about my clothes to himself," she said, sticking her tongue out.

A knock came at the hallway door. Olivier hurried over to open it while I went to the enormous wall of windows to close the heavy green drapes. What was once a room filled with sunlight became a dark room lit only by the enormous chandelier on the ceiling.

The turned had arrived.

They filed into the bigger drawing-room and found seats on the couches and chairs. I wondered where that fancy Council desk had gone.

"Good morning, everyone," I said cheerfully. Everyone except Renard looked anything but cheerful. Renard was busy making moon eyes at Olivier. "Today's lesson is staying with the times." A very soft groan went around the room. "It's important that we stay active in learning about—" More groans. "–modern technology and lingo–" Groan. "I'm sorry, is there somewhere else you'd rather be?"

"Not here?" someone suggested, earning a round of laughter from the rest of them.

"I'm sorry this isn't fun, but it's not supposed to be fun. Everything we're teaching you is important."

The turned that had spoken looked somewhere between a vagabond and a rock star. He had long brown curls, a very short beard, and clothes that might not have been brown when he bought them. But as much as he looked like a homeless person, he had an air to him that meant he thought very highly of himself. He was clearly demonstrating that right now, with his dirty shoes resting on a table that was older than his grandmother.

"Tell me something, sister," he said with a disrespectful grin. "Did you just wake up one day and decide to be boring, or were you always like that?"

Olivier's hackles rose and her fingernails started growing into claws. "You watch your tone, Randall." I waved to her to get her to calm down. I had no doubt that was how she'd been handling them in my absence. Though, I applauded that none of them were dead yet, so she hadn't done all bad.

"Randall, is it?" I addressed him. "You misunderstand something. We instruct you in everything we've learned over centuries of life so you can live centuries more."

"Blah blah blah, boring. I don't want to learn how to play nicey-nice with the villagers. I want to go live my immortal life however I want."

I crossed my arms over my chest, trying not to display exactly how much I wanted to punch him in the face. "So, what exactly were you expecting when you came here? That we'd turn you and let you go on your merry way? It doesn't work like that."

He stood up, his height towering over me, but if he was trying to intimidate me, he failed miserably. "I didn't sign up for this to be babied and controlled. That may be your idea of what being a vampire is, but it's not mine." He turned and left the room, followed by the rest of the group, except for Renard and Cameron who stayed behind.

"I should go bite his head off," Olivier grumbled.

I doubted that would help. Something was seriously wrong with the turned, and it was my job to fix it.

9

THE UNINVITED GUESTS

he turned stopped coming to their lessons. I could tell the Hunters wished they could stop coming to theirs as well, but they liked being Hunters too much to risk being kicked from the group, so they endured everything we taught them without too much grumbling.

"Hello, my name is Sally Sue. I sure like shopping at the supermarket," I said cheerfully. It was Hunter class, and we were going over how to feed from a human without them knowing. I was wearing a fluffy ruffled apron and had my hair in pigtails as part of the role play. Arthur stood next to me, his arms crossed over his chest, staring at me like he wanted to drop kick me out the window. "Arthur," I encouraged in my character's high pitched voice. "You're supposed to respond."

"You look stupid," was his answer. I waited, glaring at him with my hands on my fluffy, ruffled hips. Finally, he sighed and dropped his arms. "I knock Sally Sue out. And drag her into an alleyway."

I made a buzzing noise. "EHHH! Wrong."

He rolled his eyes, a rare move for him. "I wait until Sally Sue is near a dark corner, then I knock her out gently, feed from a spot she won't notice, and leave her somewhere comfortable until she wakes up."

I clapped, the fluffy apron sleeves bouncing up and down. "Yay! Arthur has passed discreet feeding!" No one clapped with me.

"Can we go now?" one of the Hunters groaned. I'd barely nodded before everyone piled out of the smaller drawing-room.

"It seems no one appreciates my teaching methods," I said to Olivier. She was biting her lip, trying not to laugh at my appearance. "It's okay, you can laugh. This apron is ridiculous."

"Where did you find that?" she asked while I took it off. "I need a picture." I tossed the apron in her direction so she couldn't snap a photo of me, and then I noticed Arthur was still in the room.

"Arthur," I said to him, tilting my head up to meet his icy eyes. "Do you need anything?"

He almost hesitated before answering. "I've heard whispers that the turned are being difficult. Is this a normal occurrence?" he asked, watching me pull the rubber bands from my hair and fluffing my curls out again.

"They always have grumbles," Olivier told him. "But it's never been on this scale."

"Oddities are rare for us. I hope this doesn't escalate," he said thoughtfully.

"We have it under control," I assured him, though that couldn't be farther from the truth. He still offered his services to assist us before he left, which was much more unsettling than what the turned were doing.

—⚔—

A party was in order, given everything that was going on, and Olivier decided it should be a baby shower. At first I wanted it to be just friends and in my suite, but then I remembered what Othello had said. I'd isolated myself in my own home. I couldn't keep excluding the rest of the Order. I didn't even know all of their names.

Party in the bigger drawing-room!

We set the date, sent out invitations, and bought decorations. Benjamin and Alfred grudgingly assisted with the decorating part, as did Olivier's new companion, a tiny young woman named Arabella. She was apparently a relative of Renard's, and only spoke French. Cameron kept giving her side glances while he helped me hang streamers from the chandelier.

"Arabella is pretty," I said to him casually.

"Mmm," Cameron mumbled. He met my eyes with a look I understood. Companions were on the 'no dating' list. It was very much so forbidden. If a romance was discovered, the human would be sent away and the vampire reprimanded. Renard and Olivier had been in love for thirty years but kept it absolutely on the friend level for that very reason.

"Be careful," I told Cameron while I twisted some tape around a streamer. "That's all I'll say to you."

"Me be careful? You're standing on a ladder with me and you're four months pregnant. Why are you up here? Get down, I can finish it."

"I'm pregnant, not infirmed. Even if I fell, my body would take the punishment, not the baby. That's how our bodies work. Or so the doctor says." He was the only person I could ask for advice. Well, the only one I *wanted* to ask.

"There," Olivier announced, stepping back to admire our work. "We managed to turn a hunter green room into a pastel palace. Why is this room so green? Everything is green in here. No one likes green this much."

"The cunning and ambitious do," I commented as I stepped down the ladder steps.

"There's a difference between emerald green and hunter green. One of them is pleasant. The other is not." I stuck my tongue out at her. She was right, though. This room looked awful, like old man country club awful, but now it was awash with pastels and smelled like butter mints, so that made it a little better.

Olivier checked her wristwatch. "Five minutes left. They should start arriving soon."

Benjamin and Alfred started walking towards the door, leaving once their work was done.

"Wait," I shouted, and caught up to them. "You can stay. It's not a vampire only party. You should be here." I smiled encouragingly at them. I didn't like their anti-social behavior. If I couldn't be anti-social, then neither could they.

"Is that an order," Alfred asked.

"No?" He left without another word. Benjamin stayed, showing an apologetic smile.

"He doesn't like you very much," he explained.

That hurt.

"But I've been so nice to him," I said with a pout.

Benjamin dropped his head and said quietly, "He thinks you are a demon. That's why he won't tell you his name, he thinks it will give you power over him."

"Then why did he sign up to be a companion?"

"He needed the money. His family is poor and his mother is very sick. One year of service to the devil, and they'll be fixed for life."

I scrunched my lips together at being called the devil. I was sure his superstitions came from wherever his family lived. There were legends about us all over the world. Most were incredibly unflattering and would make devil sound like a pet name. While the western world had mostly forgotten those types of horror stories, other parts of the world kept them alive and thriving.

"You'll stay?" I asked Benjamin. He nodded.

All of the Born showed up at my party. Even ones we hadn't invited.

I could say it was because vampires like parties, which was true, but everyone had a different reason for being there, and very few had the reason of liking me. Some wanted food. Some wanted gossip material. Some thought I was an oddity, the vampire no one really knew, and were eager to see what I was like.

No matter their reason, all of them eyed my belly with a wary glance.

I had a slight fear that Marie had shared Castilla's baby reading, and everyone thought my baby was a dangerous half-werewolf or something, but Olivier assured me she hadn't heard anyone mention Castilla's words. Either way, my baby shower wasn't turning out quite like I'd hoped.

My age counted for something in the respect department though, so everyone had at least brought a gift. While my guests nibbled on buttery cake and gossiped about the hostess's private life, I opened gifts fit for a royal baby. Silken embroidered baby gowns with golden buttons. Silver rattles, silver spoons, silver cups. Hand-painted trays of children playing.

Nothing was modern. Everything was based on traditions we had known centuries ago. A wooden cradle, a wooden toy horse. Teddy bears. Bonnets and booties. Cloth diapers.

Someone had even given me a handmade papoose, to carry my baby on my back.

I highly doubted that any of the handmade things had been made by the givers, but they'd put thought into what they gave me, and it warmed my heart despite the general detachment of the guests. Maybe being involved would be much easier than I thought.

Halfway through the party, the turned arrived.

They came in through the hallway door, Randall at the lead. We'd closed the drapes to accommodate Renard and Cameron, so Randall safely walked up to me where I sat in the middle of the room opening gifts.

"Randall," Olivier greeted warily. "What brings you here?"

"We heard there's a party, and we weren't invited. Well, some of us were." He nodded to Cameron and Renard with a significant glance.

"I didn't think you'd be interested," I said honestly. They had made it very clear they didn't like me. Why would I invite them to my party?

"Why not? We love parties." He grabbed a bowl of nuts and chomped on a few of them. The turned didn't need food, but they enjoyed snacks like the rest of us. "Mmm. Now those are some high-quality almonds." Othello approached Randall and grabbed the nut bowl from him.

"Excuse me," Othello said sharply. "You and the turned were not invited. Please return to the dormitory." I got up and tried to warn Othello that that wasn't a good idea, but the damage had been done.

"Oh, I see. We're not good enough for your party, is that it?" Randall shouted, purposefully trying to draw everyone's attention to our conversation. "It may have escaped your notice, but we're vampires, same as you."

"I said, the turned were not invited," Othello repeated in a huff.

"Then what are Renard and Cameron doing here?" Randall challenged. He glanced at me and grinned, and I understood. That was why he crashed the party. He had something up his sleeve, and it involved singling Renard and Cameron out.

Othello didn't notice the look on Randall's face. "You and the turned will leave immediately or I will employ Arthur and the Hunters to escort you out."

Randall held his hands up disarmingly. "Alright, we're leaving. Everyone have a nice time without us. Cameron. Renard." He nodded to them and led the rest of the turned out of the room.

Needless to say, the party was pretty much over after that.

The room cleared out faster than it takes a pot to boil. Olivier and her group took down the room while Benjamin helped me carry my gifts upstairs. An hour later, I was busy sorting through everything when Olivier burst into my rooms without knocking.

"Is that important?" she asked, gasping for air.

"Not really," I answered, setting a baby dress down.

"I need you."

That was all she said and all she needed to say. I instantly got up and followed her out the door.

"So, what's going on?" I asked when we'd hit the first-floor landing.

"A fight in the dormitory," was the answer.

"Christ," I swore under my breath. I shouldn't have been surprised, given the circumstances, but a fight in the dormitory was new. Logically, there's only so many places insubordination can progress to. Fighting was one of them.

We went down the basement stairs and I started to hear the commotion the turned were making. Shouts, groans, and scraping. From the noise, I expected to find the dormitory completely trashed, but instead, there was just a pile of them in the middle of the room. A few were still hitting each other, most had given up and were lying in a puddle of their own blood.

"What in *god's name* do you think you're doing in here?" I shouted. It was then I noticed the few turned still swinging was Renard, Randall, and Cameron. I should've guessed. "Everyone get up," I barked out. I waited patiently while the pile separated and everyone got off the floor. I pointed to one of the turned that hadn't been fighting. "You. What happened."

She looked scared under the full force of my wrath, but managed to get out, "Someone said that Cameron and Renard were getting special treatment. They said it was because of you and Olivier, and said that its because..." She swallowed and I held my breath. "Well, there were a few unflattering things said about you, and then they said it was because Renard is with Olivier, and you're with Cameron."

Now fully enraged, I let out my breath and turned back to the mass with a death glare. "Who. Who said it?" Everyone motioned to someone in the thick of the group. It was Randall, as if I was surprised. He was missing skin on several parts of his body and looked like he could barely stand up. His face was a swollen, bloody mess. I sent a side glare to Renard and Cameron, who didn't look the least bit sorry. I motioned the bloodied Randall forward. "I'll take your full explanation immediately," I demanded when he was standing in front of me. He spat blood onto the floor, being careful to miss my shoes.

"They get special treatment," he panted, his voice sounding like he had cotton in his cheeks. "You know it as well as I do."

I let out a slow and even breath because all I wanted to do was throttle him further. "Continue."

"First, Othello approving them for a turning without having to wait for the next group."

"Othello approved them because it was a special circumstance," Olivier pointed out. "They're former companions. They didn't need as much training as you did. It's like that for any companion who applies to be turned, not just them." He had the nerve to roll his eyes at her, but he put his hands up in acknowledgment of her point.

"Then there's the party you didn't invite us to," Randall

continued. "You clearly didn't think we were worth being there for it. And finally, a burning question."

I stared him down. "And that is?"

"Will they get to live here after training is over? This is a Born-exclusive Order, and it has been that way since its inception, according to your boring lectures. Will you snooty Born make an exception because they're your friends? Or will you kick them out like you will us?"

I was very careful to keep all the thoughts I was having off my face. He was right. Renard and Cameron would probably live here with special permission. I had the sway. I could make it happen. But there was something here amongst the turned that I'd been sensing for weeks. An undercurrent that was stronger than their initial grumbles. This was something they'd been discussing and complaining about for much longer than today.

I tilted my head up and looked down at Randall in a display of dominance. "Renard is mated to a Born vampire. He will live here permanently. Cameron will leave with the rest of you." Randall almost looked taken aback, but he managed to hide it under his smug grin. "I do not want to hear another word on this subject, is that understood?" He nodded. I looked up and around at everyone else. "I wasn't talking to just him."

Everyone chorused, "Yes, ma'am."

It took every ounce of self-control to not meet Cameron's eye. It wasn't because I didn't want to see the look of betrayal he probably had, though there was also that. I just couldn't afford to show him favoritism. There were scales here, and I wasn't sure what would tip them.

"Everyone is confined to the dormitory for a week as punishment for fighting," I announced. They all complained, the loudest ones being those that hadn't been in the midst of the brawl.

"But we weren't fighting!" one of them said over the rest. A high-pitched noise from Olivier shut them up. I winced and pushed a finger to my ear to comfort it.

"I don't care who was fighting," I told them. "When one of you is in trouble, you're all in trouble. That's the rule of our species. Everything you do affects all of us. If I catch any of you breaking the rules again, you'll wish my punishment was a week of dormitory confinement."

I turned, taking so much care to not look at Cameron, and left the room.

Olivier followed me, not speaking until I reached the empty kitchen. I grabbed an orange and angrily tore it in half with my hands.

"Well," Olivier said once the kitchen door had swung closed. "Thanks for grounding my boyfriend." She was only half complaining. She agreed with my punishment, though she hadn't said so.

"I hated doing that. I hated..." Though I hadn't seen Cameron's face, I could picture it, and it hurt my insides. He chose this life for me, and I'd just said he would be sent away from me. I'd broken his heart, and my own at the same moment.

"Hey," Olivier soothed. She reached for my fists and gently opened them. I'd accidentally clenched my fists around the orange halves. The floor and my hands were covered in orange juice and pulp. She took the pieces from my hands and threw them away.

"Sorry." She chose not to comment and wiped up the floor with paper towels while I rinsed my hands in the sink. "There's something off with them," I said once my hands were clean.

"I know. I can feel it too. Do you think it's getting worse?"

Frowning, I nodded as I dried my hands off. "There's unrest. But it's more than that. I'm afraid they might be organizing." I didn't have to explain how dangerous that was. Olivier instantly straightened up.

"I'll have Renard keep an eye on them. He can let us know what they're whispering."

"That'll help, but I'm sure they guard their words when he's around. For now, let's wait and see if things will die down."

And I hoped to god they would.

I'd have to face Cameron eventually and explain my actions. I didn't want him to be sent away. I wanted him here with me. I needed my brother. The number of people I considered family was very small, and I'd lost one of them forever. I didn't want to lose anyone else, but I doubted I would have much say in the matter.

The turned dormitory confinement went by quickly, which was good for me because Olivier had become a grouch without Renard around. It also meant it was time to confront Cameron, something I was not looking forward to. I was putting it off, but I ended up running into him on accident.

I'd woken up with nightmares, something that was a regular occurrence now, so I went downstairs to get something to eat. The kitchen was dark, and opening the fridge flooded it with light. I grabbed an egg and whipped up some creamy meringue, which I put in a cup and took with me outside, already dipping into it with my spoon. The moon was up in the sky, and I couldn't help but think of Knight. He should be running around as a werewolf right now, happily chasing butterflies and bunnies. But he was dead. The moon would never catch his shadow again.

Cameron was lying outside in the dark, staring up at the moon, his head propped up with his hands. I smelled him before I noticed him. For one second I considered going back inside, but I decided not to be a coward. I approached him, and after taking the last spoonful of meringue into my mouth, I set my empty cup on one of the nearby tables.

"Hi," he said without looking at me.

"Can I sit?" He shrugged, so I sat and stretched onto the ground next to him. He was silent, watching the stars and ignoring me. Finally, I sighed and said, "I can't read your mind."

"Good."

"That's polite code for please talk to me."

He scratched his nose. "I know you're sorry, so don't say it. I also know that you have more to consider than my feelings. But I'm still mad at you. Not for what you did. Because you made me feel like I wasn't important to you."

"I know. But you know that's not true," I said. "I hated doing what I did. I had no choice. There's something off with them. I can feel it. And if I'd showed you special treatment, it would've stirred the pot."

"I don't want to argue with you."

"Then don't. But you should know, I already applied for you to live here permanently. The other turned will leave and you'll stay." I hoped that would make him feel better, and maybe forgive me a little, but I was wrong.

He groaned and sat up quickly. "You don't understand. That will make it worse. You said there's something going on with them, and you're right. Right now, it's just whispers. But you do that and it'll become shouts. And you'll have a real problem when that happens."

"I can handle whispers."

"You're not handling anything." He got up and walked away.

10

OUT OF PROPORTION

At that point, during the most horrible year of my long life, I thought it couldn't get any worse. As one might suspect, I was very, very, wrong.

The Hunters completed their training course, all of them just barely making a passing grade, and they were preparing to leave the Order as soon as Othello gave them their new assignments. The turned, on the other hand, had no interest in their training. They refused to participate in anything we tried to involve them in, and because the Hunters were still here, I had a feeling Othello was delaying their departure in case we needed backup.

And the day came all too soon when we did.

My days had become much less busy, considering I had no one to teach now. Mostly I just went to the doctor's suite so I could see my little baby on the monitor. She was so big now at five months. Her head was down to normal proportions. Her fingers and toes were fully developed. I never wanted to stop seeing her little body on the screen.

Sadly, the machine turned off and I sat up. The doctor handed me more photos for my album and I left his suite. After leaving the photos in my rooms, I went to the beauty parlor on the bottom floor of the Order. It was another new thing I was trying in my attempt to be more social. I signed in and found a seat in the shampoo area while I waited.

"It's her," someone whispered. I glanced around and the other ladies in the room were staring at me. They talked in another language so I wouldn't overhear their gossip about me. They had no idea which languages I knew, and I spoke quite a few of them. Enough to know they were saying very rude things about me.

"Arabella?" I heard Olivier's voice in the doorway of the parlor. She was peeking in and looking around for the young girl. I waved to catch her attention. She walked over to me and sat in the other shampoo chair. "I can't find that girl. Whenever she sneaks off, she's always in some corner reading a book and looking wistful about life."

"Ah, to be young," I said reflectively, though also sarcastic.

Olivier rolled her eyes and surveyed the room one more time in case Arabella was hiding somewhere. Instead, she noticed the clusters of women talking about me. She looked back at me and I gave her a half smile. I expected her to lean in and offer to kill them, but instead, she reached for my hand

and gave it a squeeze, then a pat, and she stood up. "Let me know if you see her."

I didn't see Olivier again until that evening, and Arabella still hadn't been found. Renard was looking worried, so I offered to help them search for her. Cameron came as well, though he still wasn't speaking to me. Our search over the castle revealed nothing. We widened our hunt to the forest and split up in all directions. I pushed out my senses and took a deep breath as a wave of information flooded into me. I started to get a picture of the forest around me, animals, scents, and tracks, when bright bursts of light came over my eyes. I had to brace myself on the nearest tree. I felt a twinge in my power as it spiked to the level of power I had during my blood binge, and since I didn't have the blood supply to back it up, it left me weary. Focus. Just focus.

I flipped through the information I'd gotten all at once. Something caught my attention, branches that had been broken. It wasn't like we never went out here, but it was worth following. I shifted back into my own head and trudged forward. The trail led me deeper still until finally, I caught the scent of someone's blood.

Arabella's blood.

My heart stopped and my face went cold. I pulled my phone from my pocket and quickly sent a text to Cameron, Olivier, and Renard. They were too far away to hear me shout. I focused on Arabella's scent and kept going. It was getting stronger when I started hearing voices. Panicked voices. I smelled more of Arabella's blood, and it overrode my sense of smell for anything else.

I didn't stop to survey the danger, I charged head on towards the smell, bursting into a clearing where Randall and a few of his friends stood. Arabella was lying on the ground in a crumpled heap.

"We didn't..." Randall started when he saw me, his face a mask of terror and confusion.

It took me a few moments to process everything I was seeing, including the inescapable scent coming from Arabella. I was horrified. This couldn't be happening. Not here. Not now. I ran to her and lifted her head from the ground.

She was dead. She smelt of death.

My rage came quickly, my fangs dropping and my nails lengthening into claws. I had never been this angry in my entire life.

"What have you done?" I shouted at them, watching them cower before me. "WHAT HAVE YOU DONE?"

I almost attacked them. I wanted to. I wanted to sink my claws into their throats and splatter their blood on the ground. My friends arrived just in time to stop me. Olivier rushed over and screamed when she saw Arabella's lifeless body. She wailed in French, her cries of agony so intense I felt her pain seep into me. It only fueled my wrath.

"Explain what happened. NOW," I demanded with a deep growl, my fangs still down.

Randall looked shell-shocked, but he still tried to regain

his usual thoughtless attitude. "We... well we were just trying to... we didn't mean to kill her."

I looked down at his bloodied wrist and then back to Arabella's body. There was a bite mark on her neck. "You tried to change her." Randall's face confirmed it. He didn't look like he felt guilty. He was just surprised it hadn't worked.

Olivier sprang up, shouting in several different languages how stupid she thought he was, and was very descriptive about how she was going to make him pay. I held her back and she collapsed on her knees, holding my hand so tightly it hurt. "Did you ever listen to what we said to you?" she wailed. "We told you that the turned cannot change humans. We told you..." she broke off into sobs that wrenched at my soul.

I carefully took my hand back from Olivier and stood up before I walked up to Randall, grabbing him by the throat. I saw my blood red eyes reflected in his, showing just how enraged I was. I wanted to shout at him. I wanted to tell him exactly what I thought of him. How he had wasted a human life because he didn't listen to us. How his ego had destroyed Olivier and Renard's family. He was ignorant and selfish. He didn't deserve to be immortal.

But the words escaped me. Because nothing could bring her back. Not words, not punishment, and not revenge.

"Call Arthur," I said to Cameron, my eyes never leaving Randall's worthless face.

Arthur showed up quickly with the Hunters, escorting Randall and his friends to the castle. Renard carried Arabella's delicate lifeless body, and we followed behind him. Olivier couldn't stop crying. I'd never seen her like this. If nothing else from that night could've jarred me, her tears would have. Once we reached the garden, Renard placed Arabella's body on the lawn and went inside for something to place over her. He came back with a long white tablecloth, and he covered her with it. Then he came up to me, took Olivier's hands from mine, and led her inside, away from the body.

I stood outside with Cameron next to me. My fangs hadn't withdrawn yet and my mouth was starting to hurt.

"Hey," Cameron said quietly. He squeezed my arm and it calmed me down enough for my fangs to retract. As they did, my body collapsed and I fell to the ground. My throat ached with tears. I struggled to not cry. I couldn't cry. I'd cried so much that year. I didn't want to cry anymore. "Hey," Cameron said again. He gently took my arms and folded me up against him. And I let it go. I cried. I cried harder than I'd ever cried before. Cameron held me close and stroked my hair while I fell to pieces on his sweater.

"I'm sorry," I cried to him. "I'm so sorry."

He squeezed me closer. "I know. It's okay."

We stayed on the lawn for what must have been hours. While neither of us ever looked directly at where Arabella's cold body lay, it was constantly in the back of our minds. The darkness was beginning to recede when Arthur approached us, glancing at the body under the sheet as we stood to face him.

"We locked them up," he said, looking me over carefully as I wiped my eyes. "The rest of the turned were questioned. No one else was involved. Only those three." I had no doubt Othello had used mind probing on them after drinking extra blood. It was permitted in a situation like this.

"Will they get a trial? Are the Heads coming back?" I asked.

Even he looked disgusted at the prospect. "No. A crime like this does not deserve a trial. They will be executed when the sun rises."

"Good," I told him. He gave me a slight nod, and for the first time, I felt on equal footing with him. I went with Arthur to Othello's office while Cameron went to his dormitory. Othello stood with the oldest of us, including Olivier. She looked how I felt. Broken, but determined.

"Sunrise is in an hour," Othello said to us. "Lisbeth, you oversee the turned. You will supervise the execution."

"Gladly." It would give me much pleasure to push Randall into the sunlight. I didn't even bother trying to rein myself in. This was not the time for it.

The hour passed quickly, and when Arthur led the Hunters to retrieve the prisoners, everyone else gathered in the foyer. The rest of the turned stood outside on the lawn, in the safe shadow of the castle. They would watch how we handled breaking the law. Randall and his two friends, Ethan and Kent, came in. Arthur had hold of Kent, Olivier took

Ethan, and I grabbed Randall. We marched them outside, past the crowd of vampires.

Randall struggled slightly against me the closer we got to the sunlight, but I held him firmly.

"You're afraid," I whispered in his ear, pushing him forward.

"Please," he begged. "We didn't mean–"

I turned him to face me and pulled him closer by his shirt, his putrid breath turning my stomach. "You destroyed a life that was not yours to take. We respect humans. That fact is burned into our minds from the day we draw breath as vampires, whether it's from our mother's womb, or from a bite. It is the most sacred rule we follow. And you spit on that respect."

We'd reached the sunlight, a line of yellow against the black shadow cast by our home. Olivier kicked Ethan into the light without ceremony and he started screaming as his body caught fire. It took less than a minute for him to turn to ash. Arthur then pushed Kent across the line, who struggled and tried to escape. Arthur held him down as he shriveled and burnt up.

I held Randall right next to the line, as close as he could get without touching the sunlight, and I made sure it hit him just a little. Not enough to catch him on fire, just enough to make him sizzle.

"Mercy, please. Mercy," Randall sobbed, trying desperately to grab hold of me and bring himself away from the light. I might've held back if what I saw in his eyes was remorse. I would've made it easy on him. But his eyes held no shame, no repentance. Only fear for his life. For his selfish, self-centered, and miserable life.

My fangs dropped down and I scowled at him as I said one word.

"No."

I lifted him up and threw him as hard as I could. His body caught fire as it hurled towards the stone fence that surrounded our castle. He burned up just before he hit the wall, and the small pile of ashes bounced off the stones before blowing away in the wind. It was too quick. Too easy. I wasn't satisfied. But it was done.

We turned around and faced the rest of the Order.

"This is what happens when you take a human life," I shouted, my voice carrying to every ear. "There is no mercy for this crime. None. You take a human life, you die. You participate in the taking of a human life, you die. You have knowledge that another vampire is taking or has taken a human life and you tell no one, you die. I don't care how old or young you are. Born, or the turned. Important, not important. Rich or poor. I will throw your ungrateful body into the sunlight, or a meat grinder. Or both. There are no excuses, no mistakes, no accidents. One and done." I wasn't looking for a response or confirmation that I'd been heard.

In the deafening silence, I marched back to the house and everyone parted in front of me. I didn't stop walking until I was in my bedroom, and I didn't leave it for days. I lay there, feeling nothing and everything all at once. Trickles of the insanity I'd felt when I was a prisoner washed over me, and I had to chase them away.

Eventually, Cameron came and brought the doctor with him. The doctor took my pulse, listened to my daughter's heartbeat, and stressed that my mood wasn't good for the baby. Satisfied we were both okay for the moment, he left, leaving me alone with Cameron.

"You okay?" he asked.

I turned my face away. "No." I didn't feel like pretending. Not with him anyway.

He nodded and sat down on one of my chairs. "I like the new furniture. Before, your room looked like a catalog. Now it's homey." I'd traded my sophisticated style with earthy, natural pieces. He was right, it did feel homier. More lived in. Maybe I'd leave my clothes everywhere like humans did.

Cameron sat waiting for me to talk to him, but when no words came, I stood up and walked to the window. It was the same view my old room had, just from a different angle. I could see the front gate and the massive stone walls. The wind was still blowing, tossing the shrubbery around, and removing all traces of the men we'd turned to ash.

"I feel awake," I said finally. "Like I've been asleep for years and I just woke up." A dry laugh shook my chest. "Nothing brings you clarity like pain." I was drowning in pain. Angry pain. I closed my eyes and allowed myself a few seconds, just a few precious seconds, to miss Knight. Anything more and I'd start to break down again. I could picture the way he smelled, the way his breath felt on me. I imagined him holding me in his arms as I stood at my window.

I could even hear his voice in my ear.

"It's okay, Lis," Knight whispered against my neck. He was there, holding me close, his arms around my waist and shoulders. I knew he wasn't real because I couldn't smell him. He felt real, and that was enough for the moment. I put my hands to his arm and clutched his wrist like it could bring me strength. He tightened his hold on me but didn't say more. We didn't need to speak. Since he was a figment of my imagination, I didn't need to tell him anything because he already knew.

Go away, figment. You're not him. You're not real.

My eyes snapped open and the fantasy was gone. "I failed him."

"Who?" Cameron asked. I'd almost forgotten he was there.

"Knight. I never..." I turned away from the window. "I never looked for him. I never checked to see if he was really dead. At the time, just the thought of him gone was too painful. But now..."

"You need to know," Cameron finished, and I nodded. "What if he's alive? As improbable as it might be."

My hand went to my stomach. I could never face him again. I couldn't bear to think of him seeing me pregnant or holding my child. "He's not. And he wouldn't want me now if he was. An unfaithful woman."

Cameron shrugged. "You don't know that."

"He's dead," I affirmed, trying to reassure myself more than him. "But I still need to know."

That moment, with my hand on my stomach, was when I first felt my baby move. A little sensation, like a goldfish was in my belly moving around.

"She moved," I exclaimed, a spark of happiness blooming from within. "Feel, feel." Cameron put his hand on my stomach and we felt my baby's little feet kick against our palms.

Everything would be okay. It wouldn't be, I knew it. I had no illusions. But I tried to believe it, if only for that little baby inside me.

I had no idea that what we'd done to Randall would end up spiraling out of control.

11

CONNECTING WITH ICE

The castle had a blanket of quiet the next few days. It wasn't a calm quiet, or a lull in life where we had nothing to talk about. It was a silence full of unspoken emotion.

I joined Olivier, Renard, and Cameron on the back patio for lunch. Our table was overcast by the shadow of the castle to protect the turned, but it still had a large umbrella over it just in case. I sat down with my tray and unrolled my silverware. I could see each of them had a million things rolling around in their heads, but weren't ready to talk about any of it.

From the look on Renard's face, though, I knew what he was thinking. Arabella had been so young and pure, and now she was gone. He'd been very close to her, keeping in touch and visiting ever since she was born. Every time he'd gotten a

127

new photo of her, he made everyone look at it at least once. She was a beauty, with brains and a gentleness about her I rarely saw in others. Olivier knew what the money from a companion contract would do for her future, so Renard convinced Arabella to come here.

We failed her. We didn't protect her like we promised we would. That was me, the vampire who never kept a promise. Not a promise to protect someone, or a promise to keep Knight alive. I sighed heavily as I mentally hated myself for a few moments. Yes, I was going to milk my sadness for as long as I wanted to. Being immortal, I had that right. Cameron nudged me with his elbow and broke the silence.

"Hey," he said, his mouth full of noodles. He slurped them up and chewed quickly. "Did you reach out to the packs yet?"

My stomach plummeted and I felt the baby kick in response. "Umm, no not really."

Cameron gave me a disapproving look. "You chickened out, didn't you."

I stuck my tongue out at him in protest. "I did not. I haven't made my plan yet. I need to be careful. You know how the packs are about us in their territory."

"Wouldn't want one of them to get in trouble for sparing you, now would we?" Arthur said ironically, approaching the table. I raised an eyebrow at him that warned I might hit him if he kept talking. "If you need to go to the pack territory, I can take you. Hunters are allowed in certain circumstances, which is a good thing since you don't have that bracelet full of vampire teeth to protect you."

"You knew about that?" But I'd been so careful!

He rolled his eyes at me, his mouth almost quirking up. "Please. I could smell it on you." Let's hope that's all he smelled.

We left the castle together, on foot, to the Mohawk reservation. It was about ten miles away, which for humans would take several hours to trek on foot. For us, a quick sprint would reduce the time to about ten minutes.

With Arthur beside me, we took off at full speed. Another vampire nearby changed the dynamic of running. The forest unfolded in front of us, every creature, rock, and tree perfectly laid out in our minds.

I sensed his power and speed next to me, and oddly it excited me. He was more powerful than I'd thought. Running together gave us a small telepathic link so we could hunt more efficiently, and I could feel everything about him as if I was in his mind. Every sinew of his muscles, the sweat building on his skin, and he was feeling the connection as well.

Arthur's strength complimented my abilities so well, we were perfectly balanced. Almost too perfectly balanced. It brought a pull inside me, a tug towards him, wishing to feel that connection more, one we would've felt if we had hunted together in the past. I won't lie. I missed the thrill of hunting. It wasn't killing them, or even drinking from them that was fun, because both of those things were abhorrent to me now. It was chasing them as a group. Connecting with other vampires telepathically the way I was with Arthur, knowing exactly how you needed to move or compensate for the rest of the group. You moved as one, together, until you had your prey cornered and everyone could feed.

Memories of hunting with Olivier passed through my head, and I slowed down as the prey in my memory morphed into Arabella's lifeless face. Arthur immediately slowed as well and stood beside me. The telepathic link faded.

"Is the baby alright?" he asked in a worried tone, wiping the small amount of sweat from his forehead.

"She's fine," I assured him, almost flushing under his concern.

"We should keep going. We're almost to the territory line."

"Ah, so that's why I smelled dog pee," I complained, wrinkling my nose.

We walked further, passing the fence of the reservation, and were greeted by a stronger scent of urine. I had to put my hand over my mouth to block the stench.

"Is this their porta potty or something?" Breathing through my mouth only made it worse, and I tried not to gag or throw up.

"They're marking their turf. They want to make sure it will scare off other Lycans," Arthur said calmly, unaffected by the odor. Or just pretending nothing ever bothered him, as usual.

"I know, but this is just overkill. Geez." I walked faster, trying to get away from the fence and back to fresh air.

Arthur gave me that look like I was that special kind of person who looks for their phone while holding it in their hand. I pranced past him, and straight into a Lycan's claws. The pack had snuck up on us, using the overwhelming scent of wolf pee to mask their approach.

The Lycan in front of me wrapped a long-fingered hand around my throat before wrenching me to the side and bringing me against his chest. I could feel his heart pounding on my back, and his acrid scent turned my stomach. I hoped my pregnancy wouldn't make me barf on him. Blowing chunks on a Lycan would probably earn me death.

"Let her go," Arthur demanded, but he was in no position to make demands, as we were surrounded by a very large pack. By the looks of their faces, vampires as a whole hadn't made a good impression on them. "We're not here to hurt you. We just need to see your Alpha." Arthur carefully reached to pull his shirt collar back. Beneath it, right on the chest muscle over his heart, was a tattoo of a sword rune. The symbol of the vampire Hunters.

The Lycans weren't impressed.

They grabbed Arthur and dragged us away.

Being manhandled by a pack of Lycans wasn't exactly on my bucket list. Especially while six months pregnant. The one holding me loosened his grip on my neck when he noticed my belly, but he continued pulling me along with him.

At the center of the reservation village was a large open area where the rest of the pack stood. They were talking amongst themselves, turning when we were brought before them. Arthur was thrown onto the ground and held with his face to the dirt. My captor pushed me down to my knees and pulled my arm at an angle that hurt.

"Oww!" I complained, trying to get free. The Lycan back-handed me on the face. This trip was going so well.

Surprisingly, Arthur fought his captors when he saw the Lycan slap me, and several more came to hold him down but he still managed to get to his feet. "You touch her again and I'll rip your limbs off," he growled out, grunting from the effort to break free.

The group of humans and Lycans parted, and their Alpha stepped towards us. I caught his scent and recognized it. This was the pack of the pup I'd spared, and this was his Alpha, the very same that gave me his bracelet full of vampire teeth from his various kills, the bracelet that had kept me alive.

"So," the Alpha said, his voice full of authority, watching Arthur straining against the Lycans. "Two vampires caught on my territory. Are you here because you wish to die? It is my right to kill you." Arthur's struggling against the Lycans holding him down had almost gotten him free, but they had a firm hold on him and refused to budge.

"It is also our right to kill Lycans in our borders," I stated, hoping the Alpha would remember me and what I'd done for his pack. The Alpha stepped forward and grabbed me, pulling me up until I was standing. He looked at my face and I could tell he hadn't noticed who I was until that moment.

"You," he said in revelation. What passed on his face

wasn't anger or dismissal. It was respect. "Let them go," he ordered. His pack looked confused, but they obeyed. Arthur wiped dirt from his face when he got up. He looked pissed, his chest heaving, and he stepped closer to me.

"I'm a Hunter." Arthur showed his tattoo off again in an offended huff. "Your pack should've granted us safe passage."

The Alpha shrugged. "You're not broken." He turned back to me and lifted my arms to inspect my wrists. "You are not wearing my bracelet."

"I lost it," I said regretfully. "I'm sorry."

"No need to be sorry." He let me go. "I hope it protected you." I nodded. His gift had done much more than that. He flicked his wrist at the pack and they moved away. "We will talk."

The Alpha, whose name was Alexander, as I came to find, led us into his home. It was a simple, rustic structure that looked like he'd built it himself from nearby trees. I appreciated the unpolished style of the handmade wooden table and chairs he motioned for us to sit at. They were comfortable. I considered asking him to make me some for my new rooms, but that would probably never happen.

"So," he said once we'd both sat down, with Arthur insisting on sitting between me and Alexander. "What brings you to pack territory?" He offered us each a bottle of water before joining us at the head of the table. Arthur took a long swig of his, so Alexander turned his focus to me.

Now that I was here, I found it hard to form my words into a proper sentence. How would I put it? Well, I'm here to find out if my werewolf boyfriend is dead or not so I can stop feeling guilty that I cheated on him. Too much?

"I'm trying to find out some information on the where-abouts of a friend of mine." There, that was neutral enough.

Alexander raised his eyebrows. "You risked your life to ask me where your vampire friend is? Don't you keep track of your own kind."

"He's not a vampire," Arthur chimed in. He sounded insulted, like of course we'd never consult Lycans about anything that wasn't Lycan related. And maybe then, even not.

"Your friend is a Lycan," Alexander surmised.

"A werewolf," I clarified.

That made his eyebrows go even higher. "One of the Marked. I heard they found one, but I didn't believe it. And you know him? He is your friend?"

"Friend is a relative term," Arthur said sarcastically.

I turned to glare at him. "I didn't bring you here for commentary, Arthur. Shut up and drink your water." Arthur grunted and I rolled my eyes in exasperation, glancing back at Alexander. A light of understanding had passed over his face.

"The werewolf is your mate," he said. There wasn't judg-ment in his voice, surprisingly, but I caught him glancing at my belly. "His?"

"No," I affirmed. It was silly to even ask. Even if he and I had gone that far, I'd never heard of a Lycan/vampire child. Were-pire. That sounded good. No. I'd never heard of a were-pire. What would my child with Balthazar be? Vam-cubus. Incu-pire? Neither option sounded trendy.

Alexander sighed and folded his hands on the table in front of him. "I can find out his status for you." He hesitated, absently picking at a knot in the table. "They will not allow him to live," he added gently, repeating almost verbatim what everyone else had said to me. I was grateful he was trying to spare my feelings, but I was beyond that now. He glanced up at me to see if I was upset, and I stared back unblinking.

"I'm aware." He relaxed with the knowledge I wasn't about to get weepy on him. "I still need to know."

He nodded and stood up. "Very well. I will do this for you. But I am afraid this is the only boon I can give you. As much as I want to protect you because of what you did for Simon, you have lost my bracelet, and without it, my pack will not be compliant about sparing you."

Yeah, rub it in that I lost the one thing that would ensure I could enter pack territory safely to find out about Knight myself.

"I understand, and I appreciate you helping me even though I don't have it anymore," I told him sincerely.

He pushed his chair in and motioned for us to follow him out the back door. His backyard was open to the forest, and on the edge of it was a group of children playing. I instantly recognized Simon to be among them. He looked happy, kicking an old soccer ball around with his friends. He was taller now, and his hair had an extra year of growth on it. He was starting to look like a shaggy pre-teen.

"You risked death to save him," Alexander said thoughtfully, watching the children. "Even if we cannot continue to protect you, we can never repay what you did for us."

"And that's why you're helping me, isn't it? To repay me?" I didn't want to ask a favor of him if it was because of that. He might put himself at unnecessary risk out of duty.

He shook his head. "No. Information is not the same as sparing a life. One day, I hope we can make it even. And that day may come sooner than we think."

Arthur stopped staring at a crack in the window and looked up sharply. "What does that mean?"

Alexander looked like it was obvious, whatever he knew, and shocked that we were unaware of it. "There are whispers among the packs. Some of the wolves overseas have seen the vampires there acting strangely." So they had a party line about our business but not about Knight. Maybe he was kept a dirty little secret.

"Strange how?" I asked Alexander.

He shrugged. "I don't know much more than that. But if even *Lycans* notice something..."

"Then there's something wrong," Arthur finished. "Thank you, Alexander." He looked at me. "We have to go."

I turned back to Alexander who nodded and said, "I'll send a messenger when we know something about your mate. A human messenger," he added. Yes. Wouldn't want a repeat of last time.

12

CONFIRMATION OF FEARS

*A*rthur went straight to Othello's office after he escorted me home. I was mentally exhausted and went to my rooms to rest. What I really wanted was extra blood. In rare moments, like this one, I was angry at the restrictions on my blood intake. One extra mouthful wouldn't hurt me. I felt like an addict. I missed being able to drink whenever I wanted. I had total freedom outside of the Order, and now I was back to rules, and standards, and *ugh*.

Then I remembered Knight's face when I almost drained him, that moment forever burned into my perfect memory. His skin had gone pale, and his eyes almost lost their glow. I'd never been so scared in all four hundred plus years of my life. And even being so close to death, he still chose to comfort me when I started crying like a baby.

Benjamin broke through my memories when he came in

through the front door of my suite, carrying a half-eaten loaf of French bread. He took several nibbles of it before he noticed me sitting in my new rocking chair by the birdcage.

"Are you alright?" he asked me. I was used to him being kind to me, more so than Alfred, but his expression made me realize I had tears on my face. I sniffed, stood up, and wiped my face with my hands.

"Yes. I'm fine," I told him. I placed a hand on my belly, feeling a kick from my baby. She didn't like it when I was sad.

Benjamin was about to shut his bedroom door when he remembered something. "Oh, I almost forgot. They need you in Othello's office." He closed his door and that was that.

Marie gave me the death glare as I walked past her to Othello's office. I considered flipping her off, but being petty wasn't my style, so I ignored her and went straight through the enormous double doors. I expected to see Othello and Arthur in a deep discussion, but instead, there was a group of about ten vampires, all of them the oldest in the Order, Olivier included. The decision makers.

Othello looked up from his desk and stood when he saw me. "Good. You're here. Arthur insisted you rest before coming in." God, this Hunter was babying me. It was the opposite of cute, no matter what his face looked like. We might've been building rapport, somehow, but I didn't like him treating me like I was made of glass.

"I don't recall hiring him to be my nanny," I said tartly.

"Not important," Olivier said before Othello or Arthur could respond. "Clue her in."

Othello made his way to in front of his giant desk. "We looked into what the Lycan told you and Arthur." Fast work. I expected no less from them.

"And?" I asked, my stomach churning with anticipation.

"Apparently, the other Orders have been having issues with the turned. They chose to not say anything because each one thought it was only in their ranks, and it prevented us from knowing about it."

That was troubling, but it could easily be contained.

"They were told about the execution here, correct?" I asked him. That would cause unrest. It should also spark fear in them.

"Yes," Othello affirmed. "We made sure everyone was informed. And that could've started it. Especially if they were vague on the details."

"We're starting an investigation to make sure the turned are contained within each Order," Olivier told me. "But it will take time until we can safely say it's over."

"The Hunters are going to split up, a few to each Order. We'll do what we can," Arthur said, and I tried not to look at him.

"Your job, Lisbeth," Othello addressed, coming closer to me. "Olivier and yourself will need to monitor the turned here. They cannot be told what's happening in the other

Orders, nor can any of the other turned. That is paramount to this working correctly."

And then I sensed an undertone he wasn't saying out loud. That this could become serious, if it hadn't already. He saw me giving him a look of understanding, so I stayed after everyone else had been sent on their way.

"You've guessed it," he said wearily.

"Craaap," I swore, drawing the word out. "This isn't just the turned grumbling, is it."

"No. It is not." He scrubbed a hand down his face. "I don't understand it. We give them life. We choose them to become immortal. And this is how they repay us. Ungrateful. That's what they are."

"I'll do my best here," I promised. He patted my arm and walked back around his desk to sit down in his chair. I left him there to work on what could become the worst problem in our history.

Olivier was waiting for me outside Othello's office. She had on her serious face and was ready for anything.

"Game plan?" she asked me. I continued walking with her following behind me.

"Don't know yet," I admitted, chewing my lip. "We need to talk to Cameron and Renard." Keeping silent did not apply to them. Othello would've agreed. If I told him, that is.

"Agreed."

I texted Cameron to find Renard and meet us in the smaller drawing-room. They came a few minutes later, just as Olivier was finished pulling the heavy red drapes together to block the last few rays of sunlight before the sun went down.

Cameron looked from my face to Olivier's. "Something happened?"

Olivier jumped straight into it. "The turned are starting to rebel in the other Orders." While neither man looked surprised, they still looked upset.

"We don't know why yet, but we're trying to find out," I said.

Renard's gaze fell to me, and he looked grave. "We know why."

I looked away. "Those executions were necessary."

"*Non*. Not that. Though it did not help. You are the reason, Lisbeth."

That threw me. Me? What had I done? Okay, I admit, I liked throwing Randall into the sunlight and watching him burn up into a worthless pile of ash. It was heavenly. But that wasn't enough of a reason to blame me for this because he totally broke the law and deserved it.

"Why her?" Olivier asked him. I met his eyes again as he continued.

"You broke the law, and you were spared. Randall broke the law, and he was executed."

"He killed someone," I said, flabbergasted so hard I almost stuttered. "He killed Arabella. That is not the same thing as what I did."

Renard was struggling to stop tears from escaping his eyes at the sound of his niece's name. "*Je sais savoir,* I know," he spat firmly. He let out a breath, never breaking from my gaze. "But they are not me. They do not see it that way. Technically killing a human is not against the law. The law is preserving human life as much as possible. It does not say no killing. The law you broke is vastly more specific. And the turned are outraged." He lost his control over his emotions and turned away slightly, rubbing his hand over his chin to try to hide the turmoil going on inside him.

I focused on Cameron. "And you? What do you think?"

Cameron was clearly affected, but in control of himself. "I think we all agree that Randall's crime deserved death and yours didn't. But," he added. "I also think that the other turned had these thoughts long before Randall, or even you, broke any laws."

"She's a scapegoat," Olivier deduced. Cameron pointed a finger at her in confirmation. At least the turned here weren't in contact with the turned from the other Orders. That would be a bigger nightmare.

Cameron continued. "They're enraged that her life was considered more precious than his. Not just because she's older. Because she's Born, and Randall was turned. They believe they are being treated as inferior."

"That's not true," I said weakly.

He shrugged. "Just repeating."

"Any ideas how we can calm them down?" Olivier asked him.

He sighed and shrugged again. "I don't know. Honestly. They're upset. And every time they meet to talk about it, they get even more upset. It's getting bigger and bigger."

Renard had recovered enough to turn back to us. "The point of no return is near," he said, his voice scratchy. He was right. If this wasn't contained soon, it never would be.

13

VISIONS OF LOVE

I tried hard to think of how I could talk to the turned and steer them off this path. If we did that with all the turned in all the Orders, they'd stop causing trouble and things would go back to normal.

I hoped.

Olivier followed me down to the turned dormitory, but it was empty. Rows of coffins with not a soul in the room. I pushed my senses out to examine every coffin, and even the bathrooms at the end of the long chamber, but there were no vampires to be had.

I made quick work down the walkway until I got to the companion dormitory. The humans were in their living room area, watching tv and playing cards. They all stood and straightened when Olivier and I came into the room.

"Where are they?" I demanded, trying to keep my tone

less harsh than I was feeling. I wasn't about to hurt the humans, but they might try to lie about where the turned were, and I wasn't in the mood for it. "I will not tolerate lying, so tell us where they are."

An older woman looked terrified, but she spoke up. "They went for a walk."

"A walk?" Olivier questioned, like that was a ridiculous idea, going for a walk. The human's heart rate sped up.

"All of them?" I asked the woman. "That seems improbable."

Another human took the woman's hand for comfort. Her heartbeat slowed down just enough where it didn't sound like a racehorse at full speed. "They do it a lot right at sunset," said the human male holding the woman's hand. "They just go for a walk together. They come back a few hours later."

"All of them?" I repeated.

He shrugged and gulped. "Not usually all of them."

Olivier grasped my elbow to turn me away from the humans. "Why are they so afraid of us?"

I glanced back at them. They did look scared. "Because I just yelled at them?"

She shook her head. "No. They looked that way before you even spoke." I scanned the humans with my senses this time, and I saw marks and bruises on their bodies. The ultimate sign of mistreatment by their masters, for only we could make marks like the ones I was seeing. I put my hand over my mouth, trying to keep the shock hidden.

"How," I asked her between my fingers. "How could we not have seen this? *Damn it.*"

She sighed heavily and scrubbed a hand down her face. "Because we weren't looking. We expected obedience."

"We've been fools." I stepped away from her. "Pack up your things," I told the humans. "Your contracts are over. Once you're packed, I will take you to Othello's secretary to get your contract payout. Transportation into town will be provided for you."

The humans got to action, but their masters returned before they were finished packing. Olivier and I stood in the doorway, a barrier between the turned and the humans.

"Have a nice walk?" Olivier said sarcastically when the turned reached us.

It was clear that they had a new leader now, the man standing at the head of the group, looking at me like I was something he'd stepped in. He appeared as cold-hearted as Randall, though sadly more volatile. I searched my memory for his name and came up with Wyatt.

"Are we not allowed to leave the premises?" he answered, with just as much sarcasm as Olivier had offered. He tried to glance over my shoulder and saw the humans packing their things. His eyes narrowed but he managed to maintain his composure. "Did you tell our companions they could do that?"

"They've been dismissed," I informed him, moving to block his view. "You breached the contract by harming them."

He grinned in an innocent fashion. "Harm them? We did no such thing."

I took a step out of the doorway to get closer to him. "What, are you going to tell me those bruises happened on their own? That the humans are running their own little fight club down here?" I poked a finger to his chest. "I'm not stupid. And you've crossed the line. Your companion privileges are revoked indefinitely."

He grinned down at me with full confidence, even though I still had a finger against his chest. "You don't have the authority to dismiss our companions."

"Actually, I do."

"Right," he said with humor. "Because you're Born, and I'm turned. Is that it? Any Born can dismiss our companions, but I can't dismiss yours, even if you're beating it black and blue. Isn't that true?"

He had me there. He was correct.

"That's irrelevant," I said firmly, but I'd already lost my control over the situation. He twisted back to his fellow vampires and gave them a knowing look.

"Like always," he said with a practiced air. "The rules only apply to us, but not them. Never them."

I felt Olivier grab my elbow again and push me gently out of the doorway. The humans followed her, and the turned moved out of the way for them to pass.

"No response?" Wyatt said, grinning in his triumph. I gave him a long look before I followed Olivier out of the dormitory.

"This is so bad," Olivier whispered as we made our way through the castle. "Companions mistreated and we didn't even notice." Her shame matched my own. I was supposed to protect the humans here. I was failing at everything.

"They mistreated them on purpose. The turned wanted us to dismiss their companions to make a point."

"And we walked right into it," she grumbled. We explained the situation to Marie, who promptly wrote every human a check double the amount originally promised and called someone to bring a bus for them. This one time, she didn't look at me with contempt, rather that she and I were on the same level. It comforted me until the humans were all gone and she glared at me so I'd go away.

Othello was shocked when we relayed what had happened, but he informed us to all go to bed and try to salvage the situation the next day.

As Cameron and Renard had not done anything wrong, their companions had not been dismissed, and we brought them upstairs with us. I'd been decorating one for a nursery, and one for guests, in case Balthazar came back after our daughter was born, so everyone had a bed to sleep in.

I wasn't in the mood for sleep. I sat outside the massive birdcage in my living room and watched my cardinal and lovebird play together. Kanoa and Blythe. They were always happy. The horrible way my life was going didn't affect them.

Would that I were a bird, where my joy in life was sitting

on the same branch as my only friend. I knew exactly who that friend would be. The one I would never see again. He wasn't my only friend if I was being honest, but he was the only one I wanted by my side.

With my eyes closed, I consciously tried to conjure my delusion of him next to me on the plush, fawn colored carpet. What would he say about all of this?

"It's all going to hell, isn't it?"

Knight was suddenly sitting next to me on the floor. He smiled at me and I wanted to reach out and touch him, to hold him to me, but I didn't for fear it would break the fantasy. His eyes went down to my round stomach and I put my hand over it as if that would hide it from him.

"You got fat," he remarked. I wanted to smack him on the arm, but I just laughed in happiness that I could hear him be insulting again. Both times I'd seen him before I hadn't really talked to pretend Knight.

"Are you dead?" I asked him, a stupid question, but I didn't care.

He shrugged and smiled. "Am I even real?"

"Fair point," I said with a grin. My mouth curled downward and it trembled a bit as I looked him over. His hair was longer and starting to curl past his neck. Thick black shanks of it fell forward in front of his eyes, and I wanted to smooth them back. His skin looked a shade darker from being in the sun. He was wearing a faded brown and white plaid shirt with blue jeans, clothes I'd never seen him in before. His feet were bare and his toenails were caked with mud. I couldn't smell the mud or his scent, or anything of the man sitting next to me.

I wanted to tell him how much I missed him. How much I was dying inside without him. How the only thing keeping me above water was my child, but I couldn't mention her around him, even if he was just a mirage. I was still ashamed, and I couldn't bear for his eyes to no longer look at me with love. I wanted to tell him how much I needed him, how much it was destroying me inside not knowing if he was dead or not. How hard it was to live with myself after the choices I'd made.

"I'm a failure," I said finally, letting out a big breath.

"I doubt that," he replied.

"No. No, I am. I've failed the other vampires. The Born counted on me to keep the turned in line, but I failed. They're rising up everywhere. I failed the humans. I failed to protect them. And I failed..." I tightened my hand around my stomach. "I failed you."

"Are you still trying?" I looked over at him. He'd straightened up and was facing me, his gaze stern but gentle. "Have you given up?"

"No."

He gave me a small smile. "Then you haven't failed me. You promised to stay strong. That means never giving up." His optimism saddened me, and I felt even worse than I had before I'd started dreaming him up beside me. I looked away and felt tears come to my eyes.

"You're not real. You're gone."

I felt his hot breath in my ear as he planted a very real

kiss, on my cheek, and for the slightest moment I could smell his scent beside me. "I'm not."

A knock on my door brought me out of the fantasy, and the warmth on my cheek faded, as did Knight's image. I got up, wiped my cheeks, and answered the door. It was Olivier.

"Get everyone up. Othello's been taken."

14

DON'T LOOK AT ME

The news that Othello had been abducted was shocking. More than shocking. Unheard of. Like hearing that Christmas wasn't a thing anymore, or aliens had arrived on the planet. My brain simply could not process the information.

Othello was gone.

I stood in the bigger drawing-room with its hunter green walls and velvet curtains as the rest of the Born were roused from their sleep and came down for the news.

They didn't take it well.

First, we had to tell everyone he'd been abducted. Then Olivier had to describe over their shouting and talking that the turned had taken him and they were also gone. It was a two for one night.

The shouting got louder. My senses became clogged with

their fear, anxiety, anger, and shock. I could barely breathe for the emotions around me. I felt Arthur's hand on my arm to steady me, and I heaved in several big breaths. My baby's little feet came into play, kicking upwards at me to get my attention. Both helped me calm down enough to hear what everyone was saying.

"We have to get the Council back here now."

"What could they do? They're not in charge of our Order. They can't bring him back."

"We should question the humans in town. See what they know."

"Maybe someone here knows something."

"Don't be ridiculous, no one here would willingly participate in the abduction of a vampire leader."

"But the fact remains, we are leaderless."

Olivier got a word in, enough to say, "In the event of a Head being unable to do his or her job, the leadership goes to the next oldest vampire."

And that's when everyone turned to stare at me.

Yep. That's right. I was the next oldest vampire. Even Olivier was a few decades my junior. It was hard to believe that I was older than Arthur as well, but I had him beat by at least a century.

"Surely," one of them huffed, "Othello had a say in who took over his position?" Maybe Othello had appointed someone else? Please say he appointed someone else.

I thought Olivier showed great restraint in keeping her

fingers off that vampire's neck. Instead, she took a deep, dignified breath, and stared him down.

"Othello's opinion on the matter is unfortunately irrelevant. Lisbeth is the next oldest of us." I deflated in disappointment. Defeated by age. I didn't want his job. I couldn't even do my own job.

The question of 'do I have to?' almost passed my lips, but I glanced at everyone's faces around me and knew how to slip into the position of authority, even if I didn't want to. Reassurance.

I stood up, one hand on my belly and the other clenched into a fist at my side. Without me even asking, Arthur boosted me onto one of the green leather ottomans and helped me balance with my hand gripped tightly in his own. The room quieted just enough for me to speak.

"Tonight is a difficult night. I know you're all upset, and I know you're anxious for this to be resolved. We will do everything we can to find Othello and bring him back as soon as possible. And if he is lost for good, I hope..." I swallowed and noticed a quickly fading image of Knight in the back of the room. When had I conjured him back? "I hope that I can lead you with the same dedication that he did." They waited for more, but as pep talks went, that was my limit. "The Hunters will be on guard, so please go back to your rooms and get some sleep. We'll start fresh tomorrow."

All of the civilians left, leaving me standing on the ottoman feeling like a fool, still holding onto Arthur's hand in a room full of vampire Hunters. Arthur helped me down, gripping my thickened waist gently and setting my feet onto the carpet before taking a step back.

"Olivier, I need all hands on deck. We have to find Othello," I told her once I'd steadied myself. "I want every Hunter we can spare out and looking." She nodded and left with the group to delegate their task, but Arthur stayed behind, waiting for his orders. I wished I was holding his hand again.

"How am I supposed to lead them when I caused this?" I asked him, staring off in a haze at the green carpet.

"I wouldn't go that far," he commented, his tone dropping like he regretted mouthing off to me. "You didn't do anything. None of this was your fault."

Feeling weary, from more than just that night's events, I started leaving the room with him right behind me. "If I want your platitudes, I'll ask for them."

"You're assuming I care about your feelings. I have no reason to butter you up."

Stopping at the door, I turned slightly to smile up at him. "You forget, I'm your boss now. Butter away, soldier."

His mouth twitched with the effort to keep his face straight. "Fair enough."

I did not want Othello's job, as I said. I knew how to manage the turned, or I used to until they decided to go psycho and kidnap him, but I also knew enough about the Born to know that managing them, compared to the turned, was the difference between raising a pig and raising a cat. The turned being pigs that are usually docile, and the Born being cats that are preening divas. Plus, the Born liked the idea of being managed by their leader, but it didn't mean that they liked someone else making their decisions, or telling them to do things they weren't on board with. And I now had the authority to do so. I could literally tell anyone in the Order to do anything and they would have to do it. A manicure, killing someone, making me biscuits, having a tweet war with Anna Kendrick. I was the master now.

The master of the Order was lying in her bed, rubbing her ever-growing belly and staring at the embossed ceiling when there was a knock at her door. I had barely slept the night before, my mind too consumed with the knowledge that I could no longer be lazy and I'd have to actually work again. I'd have to learn how to do a job I had no experience in, and be an authority figure over people I either barely knew or disliked. Or they disliked me.

"Open the door, Lisbeth, or I'll use the master key," Olivier said from the hallway. I got up and put a robe on over my pajamas, passing Cameron on the couch still muttering Japanese swear words in his sleep, and opened the door to Olivier with a hand on her hip looking at me like I was late to my own party.

"I'm the boss now," I reminded her in a sarcastic tone. "You can't barge into my room."

"Technically, you've always been my boss, and I get your job if you're abducted too, so..." She shrugged with an excited grin so I flicked her arm with my finger. After I changed my clothes, I followed her downstairs to my new destiny.

Marie was there to greet us when we reached the business hallway that contained Othello's old office, now my office. She was blocking the way, as if I was surprised, clutching a blue folder to her chest like I was going to take it from her.

"Madam Lisbeth," Marie said respectfully. She tipped her head and did a short little curtsey bow, then she gave my simple black dress a disapproving once-over.

"I'm Madam now?" I asked her, genuinely curious since I'd never called Othello 'Master Othello.'

"Othello never preferred the prefix, but it is standard protocol for a leader." Her fingers were gripping the blue folder so tightly I could see her starting to rip it on accident.

"I prefer to not have it either if that's acceptable," I said.

She tipped her head at me again. "I was hoping..." she said quietly, her eyes darting around so she wouldn't have to look at me. "I was hoping that I could keep my position as the leader's assistant. I know that we aren't exactly close, but I've been the assistant for two hundred years, and well... I don't really know anything else."

"Ummm..." I said awkwardly. "I mean, I wasn't aware that I had the right to reassign the position?" Her silent glance was enough to say that I did. I shrugged. "I don't want anyone else. I'm not familiar with this job. One of us should know what they're doing. Might as well be you."

She smiled in relief and loosened her grip on the folder

before it could be truly torn. "Arthur has requested a meeting with you as soon as you're ready."

I glanced around the small waiting area, but he wasn't there. "Can't he just come find me?"

Marie gave me a superior look, and I could tell she was making an effort to be nice since I'd saved her job. "Your schedule doesn't work like that anymore."

Yay me.

Olivier left me to get acquainted with my new office. A quick scan of it said I would need some serious redecorating if I was, in fact, going to keep this position, which I very much so hoped not.

Marie led me up to my desk where she placed the blue folder and adjusted it until it was perfectly straight, minus the deep finger marks she'd made on one corner. "Othello left this for his successor, in case someone ever became the leader without him here."

I eyed the folder with more scrutiny than I'd had when I was staring at the finger marks. "He knew this would happen?"

"No," she said with a mournful giggle. "He was very thorough. He wanted to make sure everything would be taken care of for any scenario." She bobbed low to the carpet and twirled around before exiting my office.

I picked up the folder, opening it to find a handwritten note from Othello addressed to me.

Dear Lisbeth,

I am aware that the requirement behind writing this letter is to address it to my successor. I have no way of knowing if that will be you, however, I remain hopeful that you're the one reading this. Especially since most of what I say will not make sense to anyone else.

Change is coming to our people, whether we want it to or not. In a way, I'm glad you'll be there to guide them through it, because if any of us can, it's you. You can expertly navigate through the waters of the masses until they have all sided with you, and trust you to bring them to a safe harbor. They don't need to know whether or not you know what you're doing. All they need to know is that you believe you can come out the other side into a better world.

We are an old race. We don't like to change, even if it means our destruction. Any resistance you find should be met with confidence. If someone tells you 'we don't do it like that,' tell them, 'we do now.'

The letter was written on old, aged paper with a quill and ink, even though the wording suggested he had written it recently. Othello was nothing if not old fashioned. His words were deep and meaningful, and I didn't deserve them, but I would try my best to earn them. I opened the top drawer to my left and slipped the letter into it.

Marie burst in unannounced with Arthur right behind her. She sashayed up to me and dropped an envelope on my desk.

"Arthur is here to see you," she said smartly before turning around and going back out.

"Arthur," I said with a respectful nod to him, noting he'd gone for a more casual look with a black t-shirt that revealed the top of his Hunter tattoo.

He looked as if meeting me in Othello's office was completely normal. "I wish to remain at the Order and become your personal bodyguard."

I blinked and shook my head a few times, making sure my ears hadn't heard wrong. "You what? You hate it here. And I know you don't exactly like me either, Miss Rule Breaker and all."

He folded his hands in front of his toned body in a military business-like manner. I tried not to stare at his massive arms that were exposed with his short sleeves. "Those days are past. Your position is not safe with Othello having been abducted like that under our noses. I know how to guard someone properly, as you've seen."

He certainly did.

"Will I be on house arrest again?" I said, only half serious. The tension inside me gave just a little, knowing he would be here when I needed him. Sure, he was still a total ass, but I would need him in my corner now.

He *almost* smiled back at me. "No. But I will escort you to and from your office, as well as when you leave the castle. We'll set up a security pad on your office door so that only authorized people can get in, same with your rooms."

"I give you permission to do whatever you deem necessary to protect everyone here, not just me. And I accept your request to be my bodyguard."

He relaxed, as if he'd been afraid I would refuse his offer. "I'll bring you an itemized report of all the changes I'll be implementing."

"Good." I fiddled with my fingers and glanced down at the envelope Marie had brought. I didn't recognize the handwriting.

"Marie should be opening your mail from now on," Arthur commented when he noticed the letter.

"I'm not the president, for heaven's sake," I murmured. I picked up the envelope, a plain design like one buys in packs of 100 at the supermarket. I grabbed a fancy knife letter opener and slit it at the top, then pulled out the letter. The letter was nice paper with no letterhead, but embossed edges so it was definitely expensive. I opened it and a 2-dollar bill slid into my lap. The paper had four things written on it.

"Congratulations on your new job.

You're not seeing things.

Where does that door lead to?

Signed, Sara the Amazing."

15

SOMETHING HIDDEN

*A*t first, I was surprised she hadn't mentioned my treatment of her, but she'd always seemed the forgiving type. Then I started giggling, going back and forth between the letter and the random 2-dollar bill. I kept laughing, getting louder by the second with tears pouring down my cheeks until I noticed Olivier standing next to Arthur. I'd laughed so loud I didn't hear her coming in. I set the letter and the 2-dollar bill down on my desk and wiped my cheeks clean.

"Yes?" I asked her calmly, a few giggles trying to escape.

She raised a curved eyebrow at me so I'd know exactly how weird I was acting. "I've put out feelers for the nearby rogue vampires, in case anyone has seen the turned or Othello."

"And?"

Her gaze turned dark with irritation. "And nothing. They haven't seen anything. No one has seen anything. Not the humans, not the rogues, not anyone. The turned disappeared into thin air."

I leaned back in the enormous desk chair and thought it over for a few minutes. "What about the packs?"

Olivier and Arthur both gave me shocked looks, that I would even consider involving the Lycans in our problems. You'd think I'd just stripped naked for their horror.

I rolled my eyes at them and sighed. "Fine. Let's ignore a completely legitimate alternative to finding Othello. Who knows? Maybe one day we'll find his corpse at the bottom of the Grand Canyon."

Olivier frowned at me. "With all due respect, Madam Lisbeth, I would rather tear off my own head than side with the Lycans."

"We mean this with complete reverence for your position, but your opinion on this matter is biased," Arthur added, though with less venom than Olivier.

And there it was, my new life laid out so finely before me. People would no longer be willing to speak informally to me. It would be 'with respect' this, and 'Madam Lisbeth' that. I wanted to curse Othello's name under the burning sun for being kidnapped, and then curse myself for being the next oldest.

I slumped further into my giant chair and sighed again.

My stomach jumped a few times as if the child inside was checking to make sure I was okay. I rubbed near where the kicking was going on to reassure her, and she calmed down.

"We apologize," Arthur said with a more even tone, his eyes going to my belly as his expression tightened. "We are causing distress to your child."

My ironic laugh shook my stomach. "This entire job is causing distress to both of us." And magically, they both relaxed, the formal tone leaving the room. I rubbed my belly in thanks. "Look," I started. "I don't want you two acting like that around me. No 'Madam Lisbeth', or 'with respect.' Not when we're alone. You're both my friends." I glanced over at Arthur's stoic iciness. "Sort of," I added. "Let me pose the question again. The Lycans could help us."

"Hell no," Olivier said with a firm shake of her head. "We don't need them. We'll never need them. We can find Othello and the turned on our own."

"And if you can't?" I asked her.

Arthur crossed his hands over his chest. "Have faith in our skills."

"Fine," I answered in defeat.

The best description of my attitude about their decision was pouting. I was pouting. I couldn't say why, but I wanted relations between the vampires and Lycans to improve. Okay, fine. I could say why. Because maybe if our two species weren't so against each other, maybe Knight would still be with me. I couldn't salvage what I had had with him, but I could fix the animosity between our people in memory of it. In theory, anyway. Asking for it so soon after becoming their leader was probably not a wise choice. I was prepared to wait. I'd wait any amount of time for it to happen. As long as it did.

After a week had passed and the Hunters still hadn't found Othello. I was beginning to wonder if we ever would, since I doubted his survival was high on the turned's list of priorities. Still, no matter the odds of him returning, I was unwilling to move into his suite, which would've involved evicting Marie, nor was I going to redecorate his office just yet. The only new things in it were two letters I kept in the top drawer of my desk. The one from Othello stayed in the envelope. The one from Sara I took out every day to re-read and try to figure out what she was thinking when she wrote such a cryptic thing.

'You're not seeing things.'

Right. Of course I wasn't. Because everyone sees their dead boyfriend chilling in their room when they get really sad. Why didn't I think of that? Oh, right, because he only appeared when I wanted him to, which meant I was definitely delusional and needed therapy, or just stiffer alcohol, but that might make me see other things that weren't there, like can-can dancers, or Thomas Jefferson.

Even so, it wasn't that line of her letter that was baffling me. It was the third line.

'Where does that door lead to?'

Door? What door? Unless there was a magic door that leads to Narnia and only opened on the second Tuesday of every month, I had no idea what door she was talking about, but that was Sara for you. Half of what she said made no sense, and the other half was worth paying attention to. I figured the thing about me seeing things was the no sense part, and the door was important. That meant I had to figure it out.

So. Door. Hmm. I glanced around the room, but there was still the same number of doors as there had been the day before. Two. The double door entrance, and the one to the bathroom. No other doors. I had considered it might be a hidden door, but the wording in the note didn't suggest that. Though, taking it at face value could be a mistake.

I stood up, balanced my heavy belly with a hand over it, and walked over to the wall on my left. My fingers found no hidden switches or buttons. I continued down the wall, stopping at the large marble fireplace to rest.

I rubbed my tummy. "Little one," I said to it. "You're making me out of breath. It's embarrassing." She kicked my hand in response. I couldn't tell if she was being sassy or just liked kicking me when I talked to her. I slumped down into one of the fancy chairs by the fireplace and studied everything absently.

Othello had fancy taste, more so than I used to. The trinkets on the fireplace ranged from Hercules to butterflies, but they were all made by very famous artisans. Their appeal was who made them, not what they looked like.

There was one with rough edges in the shape of 'The Thinker.' It didn't look expensive, in fact, it was made quite cheaply. I stood up and walked over to it. While the other trinkets were made from precious metals or stone, 'The Thinker' was made from plastic. I picked it up and expected a door to open in the wall or a hidden passage behind the fireplace.

Nothing happened.

I glared at the cheap statue in disappointment and shook my finger at it as punishment. How dare you get my hopes up, you hunk of plastic? I took it with me back to my desk and set it on the wooden surface before leaning back into my chair with a huff. Stupid statue pretending to be a clue. Now I'd never find the door.

I stood up and pushed at the desk hard enough to move it, but it didn't budge. That was weird. Why would Othello bolt down his desk? There was no reason to. I studied it for a clue and noticed there were two squares on the top of the desk. They looked like decorations, just part of the desk design, but one was sunken in with a lamp on top of it.

The squares were the same size as the statue.

I picked up the model and swiped away the pile of papers blocking the square. When I placed the statue onto the square, it sunk in and made a heavy clicking sound.

This was so super awesome!!

A panel on the left wall I'd just examined clicked and

popped out. The seam was hidden with a line of wooden trim, and would never have been noticed since the rest of the room had the trim. Very clever, Othello.

So. The big question.

Where does that door lead to?

16

HISTORY LESSONS

*A*s soon as the panel popped out, I ran over and locked my office door. It'd probably be better to not be disturbed if I was dealing with secrets. Safe for now, I went back and opened the panel wider, finding behind it an actual door. And it was locked. Like, even if you found the hidden door in the first place, you still couldn't get in.

Astounding logic, Othello. Not.

I fingered the lock and considered picking it, but since Othello had gone to this much trouble, I figured it wouldn't be that simple. With that in mind, I went back to the desk and examined the statue and then the lamp in turn, which produced no key.

If I were a key, where would I be?

It would have to be a place no one would look, but easily

accessible to Othello. I thought back to every time someone other than me had been in this room since my appointment as head of the Order.

The one place no one dared touch was my chair.

I found the key in between the top part and the seat cushion, and I had to applaud Othello for his thinking skills. No one would ever look in the chair for a secret key.

I put the key in the lock and stopped. What was Othello hiding in here? Was it a slave? Was it his secret dirty magazine collection? Was it even important? Well, time to find out.

As I turned the key, the door opened before me. I stepped inside, waiting for a few seconds for my eyes to adjust before closing the door behind me. I could see the room well enough to see a cord hanging from the ceiling, so I pulled it. The secret room was a very tiny space with volumes of books on the narrow walls, a lamp table with no lamp, and a dusty armchair.

Books.

He was hiding books.

I had to pee, and I seriously was not digging this secret room of books. There were no books worth hiding like this. So why had he? Othello wasn't secretive. He was open about everything he did. This made zero sense.

Once again, I slumped down into the dusty chair and stared around in confusion. There was a book on the lamp table, and I picked it up, flipping it over in my hands. What had Othello been reading? The book was very old and the writing smudged in several places where water had stained it.

'Herein lies the account of the destruction wrought by the Born vampire, Anastasia Bathory.

There was a time when the children of the Bicus lived in harmony with one another. Lycan and vampire considered ourselves brothers. We did not fight amongst each other, or with our brothers, the Lycans. There was peace, one that was not won by war. It simply was.

That all changed when Anastasia came to power.

She was merely a fledgling, but she possessed a maturity that one would normally develop with age. She was a first-generation Born vampire, a rarity among us as the Bicus had been less and less involved in the lives of humans. Because of her heritage, her powers were beyond that of a normal Born vampire. She was empathic, and knew what you were feeling before you knew yourself. Her strength was unparalleled, and her beauty a poison that she wielded like a weapon.

Before she was even thirty years old, something occurred in her life that twisted her mind. Whatever happened to her was known to the Council, but not to he that writes this account. I know not what changed inside her, but from that moment on, she became different. Terrifying.

Eventually, she amassed an army of Lycans and overtook the vampire Orders. They slaughtered everyone they found, turned and Born alike. And when the vampires were dealt with, she turned on the Lycans and destroyed them as well.

After that, she disappeared.

We gathered together, Lycan and vampire alike, our alliance shat-

tered by one insane female. Their numbers were down to maybe fifty, and ours even less. We tried to repair the peace, but Lycans had been betrayed by one of our kind, and because of this, they declared they would execute any vampire caught within their territory. We threatened the same, and almost started another war then and there.

The Bicus appeared beside us before any more damage could be done. They announced that because of what had happened, they were finished with humans. Creating new vampires or werewolves would be banned among their kind. After the Bicus left us, we separated. The Lycans went one way, and we went another. We would never again share a home in brotherhood, and our lives were darker for it.

Every vampire that survived Anastasia's wrath was sworn to secrecy, on pain of death, about what had occurred. If another vampire ever had the inkling to do what she had done, the knowledge that it had been done before and sent us running with our tails between our legs would be enough to seal our coffin again. It was too risky.

Not only that, anyone and everyone that had ever been on her side, friends and allies alike, were executed so that they couldn't continue her reign of blood in her stead. Suffice it to say that many who had even a small inkling of feeling toward her, myself included, turned on her without blinking an eye in order to spare ourselves the pain of execution. It was not enough for some, and our numbers were reduced once more to eliminate traitors.

I have thought long and hard about what happened to Anastasia. What drove her to madness? I had known other first-generation Born vampires, and none had ever behaved as she had. I replayed every *memory, and I spoke to everyone who had survived, in secret of course. It turned up nothing, so I went further.*

Anastasia's human mother, the Countess of Bathory, was as infamous as her child. Anastasia was born when her mother was married to another man. As soon as the baby vampire took her first breath, one of us was there to pick up the child and take it back to our castle. The vampire that had been at the birthing was dead, but some of the human witnesses were not. I found them, and I used mind control to find out what happened when Anastasia was born.

The witnesses had only seen part of the birth, but they all agreed that something abnormal had happened. Something about Anastasia's birth was different than a regular Born vampire birth. And so, I reasoned that perhaps Anastasia was not a normal vampire. We had all seen her powers, her beauty, and her cruelty.

I found out nothing else about her, and though I searched the world a dozen times over, I could never find her again. Her bewitching smile and her destructive nature were lost forever. I found myself both relieved and broken to know I would never see her again.

This book is the only written account of what happened when Anastasia Bathory destroyed us. I am breaking my vow of secrecy and risking death as the result, but I have never believed in keeping it a secret. Our kind should know what happened. Everyone should know about the wrath of Anastasia Bathory.

Written by the faithful hand of James, a Born vampire.'

I don't know how long I sat there looking at the book in my hands, even after I'd finished reading it. The signature and seal at the bottom of the page confirmed that the book had been written by the James I knew, and not another less insane James that I wouldn't mind asking about it.

My memory recalled his conversation with me on the first day I'd been his slave.

"Have you ever wondered why there are so few older Born?" he'd asked me.

"Sometimes," I'd answered.

Then he'd said, *"I've often thought about it. No one really knows for sure why. There are so many rumors surrounding the topic that one can hardly discern any actual facts."* Now I was confused. Why had he said that? Maybe in his insanity he'd forgotten about her? Or maybe it was his oath. But why bring it up in the first place?

And Anastasia Bathory. I knew the name, knew even more so the story of her mother, the Countess of Bathory, a supposed serial killer of young maidens. Her daughter, it seemed, was just as ruthless.

The mysterious circumstances of Anastasia's birth stuck with me. James had penned in how different she was from other vampires. Could it be that she was the product of an Incubus and a vampire? Her mother certainly had had a lust for blood, though by all accounts she had been human. I knew well enough how much history had been altered over the centuries, it stood to reason her story had been as well.

I had too many questions, and the only person who could answer them was James. Great. That was perfect. I had to not only see the man that bit and controlled me for weeks, I had to personally invite him over. I rubbed a hand over my belly and tried to convince myself it would be worth it.

Stiff from sitting for so long, I got up, stretched enough to feel some bones pop in my neck, and put the contraband book back on the lamp table. I walked over to the door and prepared to turn the handle before I heard shouting outside it.

"Lisbeth? Lisbeth, answer this door before I break it down!" Arthur was shouting outside my office. I remembered I'd locked the office door, and I had no idea how long I'd been in the hidden room. Quickly, I pulled the light string and left the dark room. The panel clicked closed behind me when I pushed on it. I hurried over to the office door and swung it open after flipping the lock.

"You woke me up!" I shouted at Arthur. Olivier was beside him trying to stop him from denting the door, but he already had. My beautiful doors were marred with giant knuckle holes dotted in red.

"You were sleeping?" Olivier asked in utter disbelief. "We've been out here for half an hour. No one sleeps that hard."

I shrugged, looking at Arthur's bloodied fists with a frown. Why had he freaked out like that? "I do. Sometimes. Especially while pregnant. Also, you ruined my doors."

He dropped his hands to his sides in defeat. Some emotion passed across his face, and if I had to put a name to it, it was relief. "We thought you'd been taken." I almost felt bad, since he looked so uncharacteristically upset.

"I'm fine," I assured him gently. "In fact, I'm going to go back to my nap now. Did you need anything else?"

Across the hall, Marie gasped, drawing my attention to her standing next to her desk. She had her desk phone pressed to her ear, and whatever she was hearing was causing her great distress. Had they found Othello? If they had, her face said he was dead. She calmly hung up the phone with as little movement as necessary, and stood silent for a few moments, just staring off into space.

"Marie?" I asked her as calmly as I could. "Who was on the phone?"

She was very composed, in a way that was completely abnormal for her. I felt like she was about to burst into pieces. Since she hadn't answered me yet, Arthur and Olivier turned to her and were equally wary of her behavior.

"Tha..." She faltered and swallowed to clear her throat. "That was the Order Qiángdù. They had news about the Order Gennadi."

"Don and Faith are there," Olivier said, naming the Hunters Arthur had dispatched to that Order. "What happened?"

Marie finally met my eyes. "The turned attacked all of the Born there and executed them."

We were all frozen in horror.

"What about the Hunters we sent?" Olivier asked quietly.

Swallowing again, Marie met her eyes too. "There were no survivors."

17

A HARD CHOICE

*I*t seemed that every horrible event that had happened to me during that year was steadily getting worse so that each time it progressed up the scale of suck, I was at least a little prepared. Except that I wasn't prepared for this news.

An entire Order of Born vampires slaughtered.

The turned had even filmed the affair and sent it to every Order as a message which very clearly indicated that this was what they had planned for all of us.

We were in deep shit. And that was an understatement.

I paced my office trying to figure out our next move. I was tired from my pregnancy, not to mention it was well past midnight. Even though I was the head of the Order and could technically make all the decisions by myself, I still needed to pretend that the other Born had a say-so. And that meant I had to patronize their constant arguing about what we were going to do.

"We have to contact the other Orders," one commanded.

Arthur watched my pacing, wiping the blood off his hands with some tissues from my desk. "Any number of them could be compromised by now," he countered. "We have no way of knowing if the turned have overthrown more of the Orders."

"Olivier," I interrupted. "Each Order still has Hunters there, right?" She nodded. "Let's contact them. They're loyal to us, and the turned will be hard pressed to overpower them. They can help get the Born to safety."

"On it," Olivier said, whipping her phone out.

"So, all the Born are going to come here?" someone asked.

"This is the safest Order right now," I told him. "The turned are gone."

"Not all of them," he said back. Olivier froze, and I felt everyone give me a meaningful glance, indicating they had all been thinking this but hadn't vocalized it until that moment.

"No," I argued wearily. "Not them. Cameron and Renard live here." That was one thing I couldn't bear.

"No one will feel safe with them here. Not after Gennadi." What he really meant was WE don't feel safe.

Olivier looked up from her phone to scowl at the people around her. "So you're going to pin the deeds of the turned on them? They had nothing to do with anything that's happened, and all of you know it." I glanced at Arthur for his opinion on the matter.

"Cameron and Renard are on our side," he admitted, tossing the tissues away. "But..."

"But?" Olivier interrupted in a huff, whirling on him. "But??"

"If they don't feel safe, they won't come here. And then they'll be in danger," Arthur finished.

Olivier looked like she wanted to make a phone shaped dent in his skull. "And that means you'll throw out my mate just to make the other Born happy?"

"No," I repeated to him. "Cameron and Renard are non-negotiable. They stay."

I thought that my word would be final, but of course, it could never be that simple. Before I'd even sat down to rest, one of the other vampires said one phrase that summed up my future.

"It seems as if you would put your personal feelings before your position as our leader?"

Laid out very neatly in front of me were my options.

Option 1. Evict Renard and Cameron

Option 2. Evict Cameron and Renard

Once again, I had to put Cameron and Renard second, and the needs of the Order first. This really did feel like an 'us or them' thing, which was exactly what had started the turned rebellion in the first place.

Olivier finished texting the Hunters without a word or glance at me, but several meaningful scowls at Arthur. "Five of them haven't answered," she grumbled after a few minutes. "The other seven got the message. They're gathering the Born and will escape as soon as possible." She pocketed her phone and left the room without another word.

The others didn't notice her departure, or didn't care since we'd already stabbed her in the heart, me included. I was a turncoat now, so I could add that to my list of faults. As if I needed more things to feel guilty about, now I had to throw out my friends.

I dismissed the other Born until it was only Arthur and myself in the room. He stood silently by, waiting for an order, or for me to leave so he could follow me. Standing up, I braced myself with one hand on my desk and the other on my belly. Had my belly grown heavier since I'd sat down? I rubbed it and felt a responding nudge from my baby.

Now would've been the perfect time for a vision of Knight to appear and comfort me. Try as I might, he didn't appear, and I felt like a wilted rose, leaning against my desk.

"I guess this is the price I have to pay to keep my people safe." The words left my lungs like acid, burning all the way up my throat. Knight, please come. I need you. My eyes closed to stave off tears and despair, but suddenly someone was there, holding me in their arms. My heart leaped for an instant before I realized it was... Arthur.

"This never happened," he declared gently, his large hands splayed across my back. He was so warm, despite his constant frosty attitude, and I snuggled into him, trying not to think about who I was hugging. The precious few seconds in his arms was enough to put the pieces of myself back together.

I brought a hand up to rest over the sword tattoo on

his chest, covered by his black t-shirt. A feeling deep inside me was welling up, a feeling of safety and strength, one I'd only ever felt in Knight's arms, and it was making me feel something for the icy man I'd held in contempt for so long. That brought me out of his embrace and a few steps back. I cleared my throat, unwilling to meet his eyes.

"Arthur," I said with a low voice, though no one could overhear us. "I need you to do something for me when they're gone."

He responded without a single moment of hesitation. "As long as it's not illegal." Anyone else would've said that with cheek, but Arthur had no sense of humor.

I relayed what I wanted, and he approved it before we left my office, as if the hug had never happened. He followed me down the long hallway, past the kitchen, and into the entryway of the castle. Olivier had apparently gathered Cameron and Renard already, and they stood next to her amidst the other castle residents. The strength of everyone's fear, and the absolution of their glares directed at Cameron and Renard, erased any hope I'd harbored that I could somehow talk my fellow vampires out of this. Gennadi was etched into their minds forever, and their mistrust of the turned was fortified. I doubted they would ever trust the turned again.

Renard looked forlorn. His home was betraying him after all he'd done in service for us. Cameron's face was determined, and he met my eyes without sadness, only a nod of under-

185

standing for my position on the matter. It should've made me feel better, but it didn't.

I tried to speak and my voice refused to comply. My vocal cords had already given into my sorrow even if my brain did not. With a deep breath and a quick throat clear, I managed to say something.

"I regret to..." No. That sounded too formal. They were my friends. "I'm sorry, but..." That was wrong too. How could I possibly say that I was sorry when I was the one carrying this out? No one spoke up for me to finish what I had to say. I was alone. "You all know what happened at Gennadi. The massacre of Born vampires at the hands of the turned has poisoned any affection that we..." The words rose like bile that I swallowed down firmly. "...that we feel for those that would slaughter the innocent. And even though we know that the two turned housed here had nothing to do with it, the Born do not feel safe anymore. Not around the turned." I clenched my hands at my sides until I felt my nails pierce the skin. "As such, your companions have been dismissed, and you will quit this house immediately with no possessions and no financial assistance." On cue, the large double entrance doors were opened. "There's the door. You are no longer welcome here."

My eyes would no longer focus, and I couldn't see past the tears flowing down my cheeks. The sound of two pairs of shoes exiting my home echoed in my ears, and I could bear it no longer.

I wanted to yell at everyone who stood there beside me. I

wanted to ask if they felt better now. If throwing out my family somehow increased their safety, but I was tired. I was tired of this year, tired of the pain, and I wanted it to be over already. Instead of unloading all of that in front of everyone, I turned and trudged slowly up the stairs until I couldn't see their faces anymore.

18

HE'S NOT WHAT I THOUGHT

I didn't want to see anyone. Losing Cameron in such a fashion had broken me. I had no strength to face anything now. If I spent the rest of my pregnancy in bed alone, I'd be fine with it. I'd bring back the custom of the confinement before birth. I was more than familiar with solitude.

The next morning, I wasn't surprised when I heard my bedroom door open, even though I'd locked it. Who had come in, though, I had little doubt it was anyone except my former captor.

I snuggled further under the covers. "Go away," I informed the intruder. I smelled scones with cherry jam and a pot of vanilla tea. Arthur set a tray down on my nightstand, and he retreated from my bed, sitting down in the wicker reading chair I'd put next to the built-in bookcases. He glanced at the book I'd been reading, one about Djinn and weather controllers, and picked it up to read the jacket. He put it back down when he realized it was chick lit. "Get out," I ordered him.

"Eat," he countered, pointing to the tray. I reached a defiant hand out from the covers and took one of the scones, dipped it in the cherry jam, and took a large bite. It was good. Damn him. He sat in the wicker chair while I ate, saying nothing.

Eventually, I had to sit up so I could drink the tea. I dragged myself out of the tangle of blankets and pulled my long curls back into a ponytail. The tea was warm and soothing, but alas, it didn't help soothe me. Talking probably would, but it wouldn't make it better. I studied the simple white china and ran my fingernail along the bottom of it in thought.

"Did you regret it?" I asked Arthur. He looked up at me, still silent. "Did you regret killing your mate and child?"

"She broke the law," was his answer.

I took another sip. "Not what I asked." I scraped at the teacup again and set it back on the tray. "I just evicted my family. A man who means more to me than anyone here, even Olivier. And why?" I scoffed with a sigh. "I don't even have the excuse of following the law. It was because of fear. And don't think I'm not taking what the turned are doing seriously, because I am. But Cameron never betrayed us. He and Renard were loyal in their service, and still. Still. They were turned out like criminals. As if I needed more reasons to hate myself."

I slumped back against my pillows and rubbed my hands over my belly to comfort myself. Everything inside me was wishing Arthur would take me in his arms again, and the mere idea of me *wanting* that was putting me at unease. I'd just started closing my eyes again when I heard Arthur speak.

"Yes." My eyes popped open in shock. He was standing at the windows on the other side of the room so I couldn't see his face. "I regretted it." Was he crying? I would've thought it ridiculous, but this felt like a vulnerable moment for him. He'd seen me exposed emotionally, maybe I'd see him like that too. "Her blood frenzy could've been avoided."

"So you blame yourself?"

"No. Blame, no blame, it doesn't reverse what happened. But it could've been prevented. And I hated myself for betraying her for a long time. It changed who I am inside. I have no line between guilty and slightly less guilty. There's only innocent and lawbreaking. That's why Olivier left the Hunters. She couldn't follow someone who wasn't lenient." He scrubbed a hand down his jaw. "I'm not the type of person to hate who they are, but it's been a long time since I could say I liked myself. Lately though, I think I've been changing. And I'm not saying I'm completely different now, because I'm not. But I will say this. No matter how necessary it was, and I do believe it was necessary, Cameron and Renard did not deserve to be cast out like that. They were trustworthy. And I know you feel guilty about having to carry out the other vampires' wishes, but it wasn't your fault. They were in the wrong, not you."

"Thank you," I said quietly. He stiffened but he didn't turn around. "You are unabashedly honest, and while it might be one of your annoying qualities, I do admire it." I studied the curves and planes of his back, wondering what they would feel like under my hands. "I'm sorry about your mate. Causing the death of a loved one is something I can identify with."

"I'm..." he started and stopped, probably regretting what he was about to say. "I'm sorry I let the Lycans take your wolf in. I didn't know he was harmless. You can blame his death on me too. There's no need for you to carry that burden. It was me." I swung my legs over the side of the bed, intending to get up and stand beside him, or behind him, anything to be closer to that safe feeling he'd brought me. "Stay," he ordered when he heard me moving. "Stay over there." Was he so compromised that he didn't want comfort? Or maybe he didn't need comfort in the same way I did.

I hesitated, staying beside my bed, away from him. "I'm going to say something, and if you try and hold it against me later, I will deny it until my dying day." That made him turn his head slightly, enough where I could see the scar that ran down his rugged cheek. "You were doing your job. I won't blame you for it, so stop trying to be noble. It doesn't suit you."

"I did what you asked. There's something on the tray for you," he said, as if I hadn't spoken.

I noticed a small folded paper in the little flower vase. I picked it up and unfolded it to see Cameron's handwriting.

'Lisbeth,

I can't say I wasn't expecting this to happen, so don't blame yourself. In fact, I've been anticipating it for months. I knew that eventually, things would come to a head, and the Order would turn us away.

I couldn't prevent this, no matter how hard I tried, but that doesn't mean I won't stop trying. There's only one thing I can do to help, and that's infiltrating the turned ranks. I know it's dangerous. Regardless, I must do this. If this war is to happen, I'll do my part to help end it.

I'll be careful. I know we'll meet again in more peaceful days. I love you.

Cameron'

Cameron was gone. He was off risking his life trying to fix the mess others like me had made. My optimism regarding his survival was not high.

Olivier was gone. Her official reason was a more in-depth search for Othello, but I knew the real reason. She was angry at me for throwing her lover out. She hadn't said so, and perhaps it was my guilty conscience convincing me of her anger, but nevertheless, she had still left.

I was gone. With my spirit broken, I wandered around the castle day after day, feeling as if I was watching my life from a distance. I was alone now. With no friends, no family, no lover, no father-figure, or whatever Othello had been. I was utterly on my own.

Arthur was the only constant now, and we were riding that line where I wasn't sure if we were friends or if we were something else, but we had more respect for each other than we used to, and I had a feeling respect translated to something different in his mind.

My only escape was the hidden library in my office. I spent most of my free time there, reading almost every book on every shelf, and though the room was small, it had plenty of both. Some weren't in English, but I spoke many languages, and those that I didn't were easy enough to learn.

The content of said books was largely disappointing, though not dull in content. They were simply chronicles of vampires that had come before me. Tales of vampires who had built the pyramids, influenced cultures to be born, razed Rome to the ground, and many other things in history that did not surprise me in the least that vampires were behind them.

Pompeii? Vampires.

War of the roses? Vampires.

Library of Alexandria? Vampires. (Yeah, thanks for that, losers.)

It seemed my kind left destruction in our wake wherever we went. Maybe that's why Anastasia Bathory had done what she did. Karma? It was sufficiently ironic.

The volume about Anastasia's treachery was the only book in the room that was probably forbidden. I read and re-read it dozens of times, and every time I did, I became more convinced that Anastasia had been a half-Bicus half-vampire. Bi-pire. And I needed to know if that was the fate that awaited my child, a life of violence and terror.

There were two things that prevented me learning anything about her that wasn't written in the volume.

1. Anastasia had disappeared, and since I'd never heard her story in my 400+ years, I had little doubt she was still missing, or dead.

2. James was the only vampire who knew anything about her, as far as I knew, and the only one who wouldn't be upset by me asking.

Therein lay my problem. If I wanted to learn more, I would have to break two rules. I'd have to consort, again, with a vampire that disobeyed the blood limit law, not to mention biting vampires to control them, which was a horrible thing to do even if there wasn't a law about it, and I'd have to ask him to talk about a vampire of whom information regarding her was banned on pain of death.

The only way this could be accomplished was if my only ally helped me. And lucky me, that ally was a rule junkie. A rule junkie that was knocking on my door.

I set the Anastasia book back onto the lamp table and left the room quickly. It clicked shut behind me just as Arthur entered the office. He bowed in his short military manner and flicked his eyes behind me to the secret door. Had he seen it move?

"Another group has arrived," he informed me. Since

Gennadi, Born vampires had been coming in slowly from all over, seeking refuge in our home. With every larger group came a member of the Council, on which I now held a seat. "Castilla was with them."

I breathed a sigh of relief that she was unharmed. "Set her up on the top floor with the rest of the Council." Space was becoming a precious commodity now, and we had to put safety over privacy. Arthur had given up his rooms and was now bunking on my couch. Even the Council had to share their rooms with each other. It was a necessary sacrifice, but some of them acted like it was completely intolerable. I told them in the most polite way to stick it.

"Olivier sent word," Arthur said once I'd waddled over to my chair. I was hopeful and scared all at once. Was it bad news? Did she tell me to go suck blood and die? "She hasn't found Othello yet, but she thinks she has a lead. She'll update us soon." Looking away, I fiddled with my fancy feather pen. "And also, I know about the secret room with the contraband book."

I'd never been good at faking things, so my surprised, "What secret room?" had about as much effect as a 1.0 on the Richter scale. Arthur gave me the most apathetic look I'd ever seen on his blank face. He didn't even bother looking skeptical. "Okay, fine. I suck at lying."

"Yes, you do."

I narrowed my eyes at him and imagined how it would feel to strangle him. "So?"

"So?" he repeated, raising an eyebrow at me.

"Are you going to turn me into the authorities?" I asked with a gulp.

He crossed his arms over his broad chest. "It might surprise you to discover this, but you are the authorities. I answer to you."

"You're the puppy of the Council. I'm not the Council."

"No, but you're on the Council. And I signed paperwork that means my allegiance to you is surmount to any other loyalty. Including the Council," he added.

Oh. "That was in the paperwork?"

"You didn't read it," he stated, not the least bit surprised.

"There was a huge stack that day. I didn't want to read all of them," I said defensively. He let out a breath that was almost a sigh, which in Arthur speak meant he was rolling his eyes internally. I was less annoyed with his annoyance at me and more excited by the fact that he had just solved one of my problems. I leaned forward and put my elbows on my desk, then I nestled my chin in my hands and smiled at him. "So..."

His mouth twitched, the ice of his eyes about to turn me into an icicle. "Don't look at me with that face ever again."

I scowled at him and dropped my folded hands onto my desk. "Fine. I need you to do something for me. And it involves breaking the rules."

"Does in involve killing another vampire, killing a human, or not killing a Lycan?"

"Nope."

"Then done."

I hadn't expected him to be so chill with it. Now I

couldn't use the argument I'd thought up to convince him to help me. It was really good too. I'd even thought up a show tune to go along with it, though that part was just for me because he wouldn't have appreciated it.

I leaned back in my chair. "I need you to contact a vampire for me and have him brought here. Secretly. He's a lawbreaker. He indulges in blood intake, and he..." I swallowed and gripped my belly with one hand. I felt my baby's tiny hand reach out to me to give me comfort. "He bites other vampires to control them." Arthur took in a sharp breath, but remained silent. "He has information I need about... someone... and that information is forbidden to be spoken about to all who know about it, and you can be assured that there are others here that do."

While others would've protested, questioned my motives, or reported me to the Council, Arthur simply nodded his head and asked, "What's his name and where do I find him?"

19

I WON

The smallest amount of stress was off my shoulders now that Arthur knew some of my secrets and had agreed to not only keep them, but assist me in my plans. He assured me my message to James would be sent and the vampire's arrival here would be kept secret, so now all I had to worry about was being in the same room with James at some point. I wasn't sure if that would bring me to tears, or end with my fingers around his throat. Either way, I was dreading it.

Almost every Born around the globe had taken refuge at our castle. We numbered over 500, in a fortress that was made to house maybe 100. Not every human companion had made the journey with them, so we had the problem of too many vampires and not enough blood to go around. It was for that problem and many others that we had gathered for the first Council meeting since my trial, and the first where I had a seat at the ridiculous half circle desk that had magically reappeared in the bigger drawing-room.

Sitting at it as I now was, I saw that each seat had its own little area on the desk. There was a pitcher of water with a crystal glass, a little black pen cup filled with designer pens that cost more than a liver transplant, a stack of monogrammed paper (the monogram was BV for Born vampires, because pretentiousness started this entire mess so we might as well rub it in), and a vase with a single hand etched flower made of glass. Why? Because money. Ignoring all that expensiveness, the chair I was sitting in was worth any amount of money. It was like heaven under my butt. I was stealing this chair. Arthur could suck it.

Out of the other eleven Council members, nine had survived and were at the meeting. Only two had met their end at the hands of the turned.

"Lisbeth, it is good to see you again." Castilla sat in the seat next to me and shook my hand. She was smiling, but she had less of a glow to her than the last time I'd seen her. Then again, so did I. "*Su niña*," she cooed, and put a hand to my belly before I could stop her. Some of her weariness melted away and she removed her hand with a smile. "Beautiful baby. She is worried about you. She feels your fear."

Great. Didn't anyone care about keeping a baby's gender secret anymore? If this baby was born a boy, I was going to ride that boat of irony for centuries.

"The Council will come to order," Arthur shouted over

the noise of people talking. He stood with his hands crossed in front of him and waited for the room to quiet before he continued. "We have come here to discuss the current situation, and how we will proceed from here."

The Council members offered up suggestions one by one. They ranged from do nothing (who invited you?) to bargaining with the turned. Bargaining. With traitors. That would work well.

"I propose," Castilla said when it was her turn, "a full-scale assault on the turned. We find out where they are and we attack."

The smallest giggle escaped my mouth, and of course everyone heard it. I half expected Arthur to come and smack me on the face again.

"You find this amusing?" Castilla asked me, slightly insulted.

"Kind of," was my answer.

"These meetings must be taken seriously," one of the other members reproached, giving me a look like I was a five year old who had stolen his juice box.

"Oh, I am taking it seriously, believe me. But you're suggesting attacking an enemy that has double, if not triple our numbers. And triple is being generous. We turn dozens of vampires every year. And how often do we procreate? On average, once every fifteen years. We have maybe five hundred at best in this castle right now. They have thousands. Thousands." I slammed my finger onto the desk to emphasize my point. "We fight them as we are and we perish."

Castilla sat down and took a drink of her water in the expensive chalice. "You make a good argument. What is your proposal then?"

They all waited for me to wow them with my idea, which I can assure you I definitely had one, but it wasn't the awe-inspiring one they were waiting for.

"I propose an alliance with the Lycans."

The room went so silent, I could hear a rabbit running in the field outside. The sound of Castilla putting her glass down was deafening.

"You're joking, right? Having a laugh?" a Council member asked in disbelief.

"I can assure you, I'm not. They have the numbers. If they become our allies, we'll be able to defeat the turned."

"You're assuming they'll agree to it," Castilla pointed out. "Which they will not."

I shrugged. "They might. The turned threaten our safety, and in turn, the safety of the packs. If humans find out about us, it won't matter who helped who. But if we want to stay secret, we'll need them."

"This is insanity," another member declared while rubbing his forehead like it would remove this idea from his head. "Aligning with the Lycans. I know you're new here, but that's not how we do things."

Othello's letter came back to me, and I smiled.

If someone tells you 'we don't do it like that,' tell them, 'we do now.'

"Maybe it should be." I sat back and folded my hands over my belly. "But hey, we could just do nothing and be slaughtered. There's always that option." Silence around the desk, and I glanced at Arthur to see him staring at me with a look that sent shivers up my spine. I tucked some of my curls behind my ear and looked away before a flush came to my cheeks. "We'll put it to a vote. That's how things get done here, right? All in favor of surviving this with our lives by making an alliance with the Lycans before any attacks take place, raise your hands. And all those in favor for committing hara-kiri by attacking the turned with ridiculous odds, don't raise your hands." I raised my hand and felt my belly stretch with the hand of my baby. She wasn't even born and I could feel how sarcastic she was going to be.

Mentioning death and hara-kiri must've sparked something in the other members because six of them had their hands up.

I won.

The only other order of business was the issue of our human population. Still brimming with the success of my Lycan alliance, I suggested we bring back past companions that we trusted, who would never turn against us. It was unorthodox since the companion contract was binding, and had more than a few words about our non-involvement in their lives after they left us, but desperate times and all that jazz. We had more than enough money to make up for bending the rules, and now was not the time to be caring about social issues.

After the meeting ended, messengers were dispatched to the Lycans, and the dismissed companions we chose were contacted. I was officially breaking two codes of conduct while still being an unofficial leader. Or maybe I was official now? Was there a waiting period for being official when you get the job from a kidnapping? Was it like a human marriage where the person has to be missing for seven years before you can get married again? No one had said anything, so maybe I was officially official until Othello came back.

If. If Othello came back.

A week after the Council meeting, Arthur knocked on the doorway of the secret room, preventing me from nodding off in the dusty chair. I glared at him and thumped the Anastasia book onto the end table before reaching a hand out for him to take. He crossed from the doorway to where I sat and helped me out of the chair. My belly had greatly increased in size, and even though it pained my dignity, getting in and out of chairs now required Arthur's assistance. I didn't thank him for helping because that meant every other phrase coming out of my mouth would be 'thank you', and he didn't require gratitude to continue doing so.

"God, my feet hurt," I groaned out. "Any chance being my underling involves foot rubs?" I waddled out of the hidden room and heard Arthur close the door behind us. He followed me to one of the chairs by the fireplace and helped me sit down before sitting in front of me. What was he doing?

"Now," I said when I'd finally found a position in the chair that was mildly comfortable. "Why did you pull me out of my hideaway? I was about to take a nap. I'm pregnant. I like naps."

"Several things require your attention, I'm afraid. You'll have to nap later," he said with a hint of sarcasm. I shut my eyes, still feeling a bit sleepy, and then Arthur's hands were on my feet, slowly removing my slip-on shoes.

"What are you–" His hands pressed into the swollen skin of my left foot and I moaned loudly in relief. He hit the right spots, massaging away all the aches until I was putty beneath his fingers. His hands moved to my ankles, then up my calves.

"Hands." I popped one eye open to see him kneeling between my knees. I lifted my hands from the armrests and slid them into his rough palms, and he started massaging them too. I groaned again and leaned my head onto the back of the chair. "You'd be surprised how much tension people carry in their hands," he said while his fingers worked over my palm.

"Please tell me you're not giving me a hand massage just so I can sign a bunch of papers."

He made a noise that was *almost* a chuckle. "No. I do have papers for you to sign, but that's not why I'm doing this."

I sighed comically. "Do I have to get up?"

"Not yet."

I let out another mewl when he pressed onto my thumb pad. "Awesome." He finished with my hands and he bent over me, picking me up from the chair. "The hell are you doing?" He walked me over to a couch on the other side of the room and set me on it before sitting behind me.

"This'll be better if you stop complaining," he snarked as his fingers pressed into my spine. Delicious, relaxing sensations went up my back, and he hit all the right spots there too.

"I think you've been holding out on me," I groaned out, leaning into his hands.

His warm breath was on my shoulder. "Maybe I wasn't sure you would let me massage you without you thinking I was trying to get some."

Another sigh escaped my lips. "Even if you were, I'd let you." *What.* Why did I say that? Curse you Arthur and your magic fingers! His hands stilled from my words, making me turn to look at him. "I didn't mean–"

Without wasting another moment, Arthur brought one hand to my neck and pulled me to him, kissing me delicately on the lips like I was a piece of fine china he didn't want to shatter. With me unable to process this, he kissed me again and I stared up into his icy blue eyes.

"I love Knight," I said feebly. And I meant it. Dead or alive, he would always be my mate. Would there be room in my heart for another?

"I know," Arthur said, and he pressed a tender kiss to my forehead. "If he is alive, I will fade into the background and we'll never speak of this again." He kissed my cheek. "And if we discover he's truly gone..." As used to the idea as I was, it still brought a single tear down my cheek. "Maybe things can change between us."

I sniffed and he swiped the tear away. "But you hate me."

A small smile curled up on his face and my heart skipped a beat at the sight of it. "I did. But then I learned to respect you. And now..." His thumb ran up my jawline. "You are infuriatingly amazing."

"Thanks?" He smiled again and I wanted to kiss those lips one more time, but he let me go and stood up.

"Kiss me again." The words slipped out and my cheeks pinkened at how willing I was to care for him after all we'd been through.

"No," he said gently, making me pout. "This is all I can give you until we find out about Knight. And I was serious before. If he's alive, this never happened. I'm not saying that to hurt you, so please don't think that." I shook my head, because I understood, and he relented, leaning over me. "One more kiss, and then I have to slip back to my role beside you. For now."

The kiss he gave me was endless, tender, and made my broken heart feel a little less shattered.

The next day, Arthur arrived in my office, and with one look I knew he had indeed slipped back into being my underling. I won't pretend I wasn't sad about it, but I can't say I was eager to learn of Knight's demise, just so I could be in Arthur's arms again. There was no choice between the two. Not even a little. I'd choose Knight every time, and Arthur knew it.

"Paperwork?" I asked him with a smile. Nodding, he

handed me a stack of papers to sign, and its thickness was causing phantom pains in my wrist just looking at it.

"These are the temporary companion contracts made for the returning companions."

"That was fast," I commented in surprise while lifting up the first one. I scanned it and found it very well thought out with very in-depth legal language. "Do we... Is there a group of vampire lawyers here that write these?"

Arthur rolled his eyes at me in the exact fashion Olivier always did, like I was the stupid cousin he had to babysit all the time. "For a smart person, you are very short sighted." This coming from the man who had kissed me senseless only a day before.

I stuck my tongue out at him. "There's a difference between being smart and not paying attention."

"Yes, I'm sure you're very adept at making that distinction." I threw a paperweight at him, which he caught insultingly with little effort. "I noticed you didn't contact any of your past companions."

"Well, Cameron is a vampire now, one runs his own vineyard, and the rest have lives and obligations like humans are supposed to. I wanted the best for them, and that's what they did. They got the best. That means they're too busy to help us, which makes me very happy."

"And the one with the vineyard?"

"He would come if I asked, which is why I won't do it. I won't bring him back here to see us in shambles. I couldn't bear it."

"Speaking of which," Arthur murmured. I glanced up at him, hoping he might reconsider about the no kissing thing, but he merely added another signed contract to the stack on my right. "He's here."

He? He who? Cameron? Othello? ...Knight?

I felt my pulse begin to race and my hope lifted that it might be Knight, stupid as it was. Maybe Alexander had found him and simply sent him to me to cut out the middleman.

Arthur saw the look on my face and shook his head slightly, making me wilt into my chair. "I'm afraid it's a guest you're not looking forward to seeing. James is here."

20

A FAMILIAR FACE

My feet struggled to move forward on the plush red carpet that led to the bigger drawing-room. I stopped at the door, my hands clutching the Anastasia book in a sweaty mess. I reached out for the door handle. My hand shook every second until it landed on the cold metal. I gripped it tightly and stood there, hoping the door would open by itself so I wouldn't have to do it.

"He bit you," Arthur stated. He knew. He'd known this entire time, even when I mentioned James liked doing that to other vampires, and he never said anything.

"You questioned him when you were hunting me?"

"Yes and no. Yes, I questioned him. No, he didn't tell me about it. I figured it out. Your behavior, certain things you've said, and as if I didn't need confirmation, you're scared to death to open that door because he's behind it." I dropped my hand and felt my cheeks redden. The shame of being bitten was still there, as if I felt somehow that it happened because I didn't stop him or didn't try. Like it was my fault. "You're safe." I looked up at him, his gaze steadfast as always. Slowly, he leaned in and kissed my forehead, steadying me just enough. "I won't let him bite you." He stepped back and I nodded to him, pushing the doors open.

My gaze immediately found James amongst the three people that stood in the middle of the hunter green room. With his back turned, he was admiring one of the large paintings on the wall and pointing at it while saying something to the woman next to him. The woman was Sara, with her pink-tipped hair that was longer now and in stylish waves. She wore a golden dress that looked like it belonged to an Egyptian goddess, emphasizing her generous curves. The third person was James's son, Drake, whom I was not expecting to see. His presence still confused me with his human not-human smell. He saw me first and pat James on the arm to get his attention.

My breath left my lungs as James turned to me with a weak smile. His pallor was diminished and his eyes had sunken in so badly he looked like a drug addict. More importantly than that, that implacable air of superiority I had come to know was no longer in his eyes. This was not the James that had bitten me. This was the James that had written the book in my hands. The one before his binge filled madness, before his insanity, and before his cruelty.

"Hello, Lisbeth," he said softly.

The sound of his voice sparked fear inside me again, just

barely lessened by the fact that his voice was thin and broken. I couldn't find words to respond because I hardly knew where to begin. Sara still had her back turned, and my guilty conscience wondered if she hated me now, after how I'd treated her. I hadn't even bothered to feel bad about it at the time because I hadn't realized what I'd done until much later. I tried to call her name, but my voice faltered so I ended up squeaking in her direction.

"What'd you use the 2-dollar bill on?" she asked finally.

I laughed and sobbed all at once. "Pencils."

She turned and raised an eyebrow at me. "Seriously? Pencils? They'd better be nice pencils." I tried to convey my despair over what I'd done to her with only the look on my face, because if I started apologizing, James might try apologizing too, and I didn't know what I'd do if he did. Yell? Probably.

It went quiet again and I stole a glance at James's pale face. I couldn't stop my stomach from twisting into a knot when he met my gaze.

"I assume we're here because of that." He gestured to the book I had in my hands.

I found my voice finally, saying, "I need information on Anastasia."

"That information is forbidden," he said, sliding his eyes to Arthur in a challenge, but the warrior was silent. "How do I know you won't have him arrest me if I even speak one word about her?"

"If this was a trick, you wouldn't have come," I told him. "Sara would've told you."

"Maybe," she said with a grin. "Or maybe I'd get him locked up so he'd behave himself." James grinned back at her and took her hand in his.

Oh.

The shock at the sight of their intertwined hands froze me. A human and a vampire. I mean, Olivier and Renard had been in love for thirty years prior to his being turned, but they kept it strictly platonic. I had a feeling these two had no such qualms. Me loving a werewolf was high on the ick factor. Human plus vampire was not on the ick factor. It was on the 'you have disgraced your family and your cow' factor.

"I'll tell you everything I know, on one condition," James said. He kissed Sara's hand and let it go, stepping closer to me. "If you forgive me for what I did to you."

No. That was too much, far too much.

"No. There will be no forgiveness," I said firmly, every step of his shoes forming a cold terror inside me, and I felt a slight pain in my belly.

"Please, Lisbeth. I've treated many people badly in my lifetime, but I've never treated anyone as horribly as I did you." I couldn't breathe. The more he spoke, the more he sounded like the old James, and the more he spoke about what he'd done, the more my mind conjured up the memories. The agony, the torture, and all the enjoyment he'd gotten from it.

Trying to catch my breath, I ground my teeth together. "I

said no, James. Respect when someone says no, for once in your life."

"Lisbeth," James pleaded, just before he reached out and put his hand on my arm.

I screamed in white-hot agony that burned through me like the surface of the sun. With his hand on my arm, I could feel remnants of the connection his bite had made, even though it had long been destroyed. I felt sick and frightened all at once, recoiling as something splashed against my legs. Arthur was there to stop me from falling, and he picked me up, rushing me out of the room.

My ear against his chest, I felt the rapid beating of his heart as adrenaline rushed through his system. "No, I need..." Pain ripped across my stomach and he almost faltered in his path across our home. "I need to ask him about Anastasia."

He went up the stairs, taking them three at a time, my head bouncing against him. "Your water broke. You've gone in labor."

21

I WAS WRONG

I was too early. My baby wasn't due for another month.

"It's too soon," I protested weakly from Arthur's arms. "We're supposed to meet with the Lycans today, I can't miss the summit." He kicked the door open to the waiting room in the clinic wing, and the nurse hopped up from her desk, coming over to close the door behind us. "It's too soon," I repeated to her. Arthur refused to set me down as she guided us to the delivery room.

"Vampire babies come early. Nothing to worry about," she comforted, looking back at me.

"That wasn't in the baby books," I joked with a wince. My stomach was tightening up and it did not feel pleasant. "My stomach. Oww." I pointed to it. The nurse had the nerve to chuckle at me as she helped Arthur place me onto the bed in the delivery room. Haha, look at the cute vampire that's having a contraction. I will cut you.

"It's just a contraction," Arthur informed me, like a twit. He helped situate my pillows so I could lean back.

"Shouldn't the father be here?" the nurse asked as she put a few pulse monitors on my belly.

I laughed dryly at her, wincing. "He's not exactly the showing up kind of person."

"I'll get the doctor," the nurse said when she was halfway out the door.

The pain subsided and I focused on breathing evenly, coming out of it to find I was holding Arthur's hand. He leaned in and kissed my sweaty forehead, but the moment was ruined because as if on cue, a highly potent scent of lilacs washed over me, and I almost barfed all over Balthazar when he appeared next to me.

"Am I late? Is she here?" he asked, looking around for the baby.

"You!" I shouted at him in a rage. "You weasel-faced giant-eared moron —owww— how dare you just show up at the last minute —owww!" I grabbed his hand to combat another contraction and squeezed it extra hard to make sure he knew how pissed off I was. When it passed, I slapped his arms several times in punishment while he tried to fend me off.

"I'm sorry, Lisbeth! I really did try to get here before now. Time moves differently in my homeland." I continued my assault on his arms. "One hour there could mean a month here. And vice versa. It's unpredictable."

"Don't you make excuses, you walking pheromone factory! You've been gone for months! I've been by myself. I've been alone." I broke out into a sob.

"I won't leave you again," he promised. "I swear, you won't raise our baby alone."

The doctor chose that moment to come in, just as another contraction hit me. Behind him was Benjamin and Alfred, who took a seat on the plastic couch opposite the bed.

"Lisbeth, how lovely to see you again," the doctor said pleasantly, like I wasn't in labor. I tried to smile at him through the pain, but it turned out more like a grimace. "Ah, your Incubus friend is here." He nodded to Balthazar in respect.

"How long do you −oww− think I'll be in labor? I kind of have things to −oww− do. The summit is this afternoon."

He chuckled at me too, because I was just so super adorable in my pain. I will cut you as well. "Vampire labor is unpredictable. It's not like human births, but vampire babies still come out at their own schedule. It could be an hour, it could be five hours."

After his comforting words, the nurse helped me change into a hospital robe. With the five men in the room facing the other way for it, I realized all of them would be there when I had to start pushing.

"There are *way* too many men in this room," I grumbled. The doctor wheeled in two metal stands with IV lines hanging off them, and the nurse brought in an electric cooler with blood which she plugged into the wall.

"For them," the doctor explained, pointing to Benjamin and Alfred. As soon as my baby was born, I would need to feed to replenish my blood supply and repair my body, and it would require a lot more blood than I normally needed. As per the contract they'd signed, that would be the last time I was allowed to feed from them. There was also a clause about me potentially drinking too much, which could kill them.

The nurse hooked me up to some machines and studied the read-out for several minutes until declaring we still had a long way to go, which was confirmed by a pelvic check that I made the men turn away for.

Only one to five hours to go.

I was tired. I was starving. I was more excited at the prospect of a cheeseburger than seeing my baby for the first time. I jest. I would happily hold my daughter in my arms while eating a cheeseburger.

Funnily, even though I was in pain every few minutes, that wasn't the worst part of it. No, the worst part was Marie, and every other vampire that barged in unannounced like I was simply knitting a blanket or cooking dinner, and all they had to tell me was that this had happened, and that needed my signature, as if this entire Order couldn't function without my presence.

After I cut the nurse, doctor, and everyone else who

strolled into this room, I was going to kill Othello for being kidnapped like a sap and sticking me with this crap job.

Balthazar dutifully mopped my forehead of sweat and planted a kiss on my clammy skin. "You're doing good, sweetheart."

"Madam Lisbeth," Marie said from the doorway.

"I swear to god, get the hell out of here, Marie! If you interrupt us one more time, you're fired!" I clawed at Balthazar's hand to get through another contraction.

"What is it?" Arthur asked her before she could leave.

"Well, ummm..." She hesitated under my glare. "The Alphas have arrived."

"The what?" I panted in confusion.

"The Lycans," Arthur explained, squeezing my hand in his. "The summit is about to start." Of course, I knew exactly what he was talking about, but my brain was addled with pain.

I whimpered, exhausted, and wishing this would all be over already. "I can't miss the summit, Arthur. I can't..." Everything inside me felt weak, defeated, vulnerable. Arthur knelt beside my bed and brushed the wet strands of my hair from my forehead. "I have to bring the Lycans back to our side. For him. For Knight. No one else can win them over, no one else cares like I do."

"Then you only have one option," he said, leaning in for one last kiss to my forehead.

"Push that baby out right now so we don't keep them waiting?" I joked with a wince. He made a face like, sure that works for me.

It was time to focus. This baby was coming out right now whether she liked it or not, because I wasn't going to miss the meeting that would change the fate of my world for anything. I closed my eyes and breathed deeply, conjuring up the powers I had during the blood binge. It was difficult without the extra blood to support it, but I managed to connect with the baby inside me. I saw glimpses of her tiny body inside my womb and felt her coo to herself from the feeling of me connecting to her.

"Baby," I said out loud, speaking to her directly. "It's time to come out." I felt her respond with a wiggle, and then the pain intensified, pushing me out of her energy and back into mine. It was safe to say that what I'd done had worked. Within minutes, I was standing on the cold tile with Arthur and Balthazar's hands holding me upright, and the doctor kneeling in front of me.

Push. Push.

The more I pushed, the more my hunger grew. The smell of human blood flowing through Benjamin and Alfred's veins started to override everything else.

"Focus, Lisbeth," Arthur said as he gripped my hand. "Focus on the baby. Don't let yourself go into a frenzy." His words made me realize how close I was to it. My fangs dropped and I felt the tendrils of a frenzy begin to grab me.

The doctor slapped my thigh a few times because I'd stopped pushing. It wasn't enough to hurt, but it brought me back to my task. "Push," he ordered in a shout.

I pushed the blood hunger away with memories of the

ultrasounds, her tiny little hands and feet that she liked to stick into her mouth. I held onto those moments when the pain rose in waves until there was nothing but my screams to keep me from going mad.

And then...

A different scream entered the room. A high-pitched wail came from beneath me, and the pressure subsided, making me weak at the knees. The doctor wrapped up what he held in his hands and handed it to the nurse. I couldn't focus on that little lusty cry that got further and further away. I couldn't even remember what I was doing or where I was.

"Hold her," the man in front of me said. I felt two arms intertwine with mine until I couldn't lift them. The man took a bag of blood out of a white cooler, stuck a straw in it, and held it to my lips. "Drink." I recoiled from the smell. I didn't want bagged blood. I wanted to drink from a human. He forced the straw past my lips and squeezed the bag enough so some of the blood entered my mouth. At the taste of it, I didn't care that it was gross. I sucked on the straw until it made that annoying noise that meant the bag was empty. The man took the bag away and threw it in a bin. He turned back to me and inspected my eyes, then nodded to whoever was holding my arms. They loosened their grip enough to where I could move.

With the blood seeping into my system, I remembered the doctor and the two men holding my arms. Everything came back slowly, including the little cries I could still hear. I tried to get away so I could find her, but the doctor and the hands on my arms stopped me.

"You have to feed first," he told me.

Alfred and Benjamin were standing next to the plastic couch, waiting for me to feed from them for the last time. The doctor took one last look at my eyes, and with another nod, Arthur and Balthazar let me go.

The doctor had explained to me along the way that a blood frenzy could happen from the loss of blood and the damage to my body, and I'd foolishly thought it wouldn't happen to me. I was almost embarrassed, but the doctor's face showed no judgments. He knew it could happen, and he had been prepared.

I fed from Alfred first. My fangs sunk into his deep, chocolate skin, and with every sip, I felt less weary. The pain below my waist got duller but didn't disappear before the doctor put his hand on my arm to stop me. Benjamin was next, and he hugged me with a smile before I sunk my teeth into his soft neck. Any pain I felt was gone long before the doctor stopped me again.

Alfred and Benjamin left after giving their farewells, and the doctor stayed to clean the room while I took the quickest shower ever down the hall and put on a simple black dress and jacket. Balthazar gripped my hand with a smile when I came out of the bathroom. The doctor had finished cleaning and was standing with Arthur next to an open door on the other side of the hallway. I could hear soft cries coming out of that room, and I almost let go of Balthazar's hand in my haste to go through the doorway.

The nurse stood in the middle of the nursery room holding a little white bundle of blankets. The room had two cribs on one end, and a counter with a baby scale and changing station on the other. The blankets started to wiggle in the nurse's arms, making fitful cries of frustration. I walked closer until the bundle of blankets revealed a tiny, pink head covered in black curls.

The nurse turned to me and smiled. "Meet your daughter, Lisbeth."

Daughter. My daughter. She was finally here.

My daughter looked up at me and stopped fussing when she saw my face. I took her from the nurse and held her close to my chest. She was so warm and so tiny.

"Here," the nurse said as she handed me a bottle full of blood. "Maybe you can get her to drink." I pushed the bottle close to my baby's face, causing her to start crying again. I tried several more times with the same result, and the nurse motioned for the doctor to come closer. "She should be feeding. She's turning the bottle away."

My natural response to the doctor bending over my baby's head was to pull her closer to my body and move away from him. All of my fears came bubbling up, and I cast a worried glance at Balthazar and Arthur. My bi-pire baby wasn't normal. Would they take her away from me? Would she be destroyed out of fear?

"We need to examine her, Lisbeth," the doctor soothed, holding his hands out for my baby.

That's when my daughter bit into my chest.

⊶⊷

My initial cry of pain didn't register in the doctor's plan to take her from me until the blanket slipped and he saw her fang deep in my breast. From his reaction, you'd think I was holding a nuclear bomb instead of a baby.

"She's... she's drinking vampire blood," the nurse exclaimed in horror.

"What is she?" The doctor was staying a safe distance away, in case the newborn baby decided to attack him.

Balthazar stepped in front of us, Arthur coming beside me to put a hand on my shoulder, both of them ready to protect us. "She's my daughter," Balthazar warned with a tone that made even me a little frightened. "I promise you, if you harm her, you won't enjoy what I will do to you."

"You had a child with an Incubus?" the doctor asked in disbelief and shock. "We thought she was Othello's." *Seriously?* I rolled my eyes.

My baby finished drinking, pulling away from my breast, and I caught the drop of blood on her lip and wiped it on the blanket, then hoisted her to my shoulder for a burp, which she provided obligingly.

"It seems bi-pires drink vampire blood. It doesn't mean she'll attack us. She's a baby," Arthur pointed out. I almost laughed that he'd also come up with the word bi-pire. It didn't comfort the doctor and nurse, but they moved closer from the other side of the room, edging towards the unknown baby.

I looked down at her again and found her studying me. She had a little stubby nose and chubby cheeks. Her swollen eyes were open as wide as they could go. They were blue on the outside and purple on the inside, a perfect mix of her parents' eye colors.

She was perfect.

"Madam Lisbeth," Marie's voice burst into the doorway.

I stopped myself from yelling at her so I wouldn't startle the baby. "Yes?" I hissed in a whisper.

"The summit is starting." She looked at the baby in my arms. "Congratulations, by the way."

"She's not Othello's," I told her, putting my baby against my shoulder.

Marie smiled at me. "I know."

I thanked the doctor and nurse, and Balthazar gave them warning looks with a protective hand on my back. "Down, boy," I warned him when we left the clinic wing.

"They're all going to react that way. You might need us to threaten everyone's lives again," Arthur pointed out.

"I won't let them hurt her," Balthazar promised. I held her closer to me and felt her tiny warm breath on my chest.

"You're mistaken," I told them as we walked down the hall. "If anyone hurts her, they won't have to worry about either of you. I'll kill them before their next breath leaves their lungs." I adjusted my baby in my arms and squared my shoulders, giving Arthur a smile. The warmth that built in my chest at the sight of his face gave me hope. Hope that maybe someday the pain of losing Knight wouldn't overwhelm my every thought, and I'd find a way to live again. I wasn't sure how Arthur fit into that, or how I felt about him, but maybe it would work itself out with time. Especially if there was more kissing involved.

"Let's form the Lycan alliance, gentlemen." They followed me down the hallway until we reached the bigger drawing-room.

I stopped suddenly. Something was invading my nose, and I couldn't put my finger on what it was, but my body certainly knew it was worth alerting me. I shook it off and kept walking.

The closer I got to the bigger drawing-room, the more alarms were going off in my head. Balthazar took the baby from my hands when we got to the doors, and Arthur opened them for me.

The hunter green room was filled to the brim with vampires and Lycans. The scents of both canceled themselves out in my senses so that I barely smelled anyone in the room, but I still felt that something was off. It was clear that I was late when everyone turned to me and stopped talking.

I saw James, Sara, and Drake in the corner of my eye, and Sara waved to me, then pointed to somewhere in the crowd. She was gesturing to the group of Alphas standing in the area surrounding the half circle desk. I recognized Alexander and Jesse from their ranks.

Castilla came up to me and kissed me on both cheeks, but I couldn't take my eyes off the group of Alphas. "*Felicitaciones*," Castilla said. "Congratulations on your little *niña*. I'm so sorry we had to pull you away from her so soon."

"It's fine," I said in auto-response. Jesse waved to me and motioned behind him.

Someone came from deep in the group of Alphas, and they all parted to let him pass.

My heart stopped when I saw a face emerge among them that I thought was lost to me forever, and the truth of the moment came crashing down on me like an atomic bomb, destroying my reality in one fell swoop.

Knight was alive.

NOTES

3. BECOMING A DOLPHIN

1. onee-san: Older sister

6. TECHNICALITIES

1. Okaa-san: Mother

Glossary

*B*icus: A collective term for the sibling creatures known as Incubus and Succubus.

Bonding ceremony: A vampire wedding involving a vow between the couple, exchanging of each other's blood, and mixing their blood together through a cut on their wrists.

Born vampires: The product of an Incubus and human female union. They can turn humans, create drones, and give birth to new vampires. Born vampires must drink fresh human blood every day. Drinking bagged human blood cannot sustain them and will cause them to slowly starve.

Companion: A term for the humans that serve vampires. They sign a ten year contract and are chosen by a vampire to live in their rooms, and be willingly bitten once a day to feed the vampire. Once their contract is up they can either renew it, or they can leave with a promised sum of money upon contract termination.

Council: A group comprised of the heads of each vampire Order. They oversee all vampires, pass judgement for infractions, and direct the vampire Hunters.

Dhampir: The product of a vampire and human union. None were known to exist as the two species typically do not mix romantically.

Frenzy: A state vampires reach when they are so starved of blood their body can no longer cope. They become wild, their eyes glow red, and they will attack until their hunger is sated.

Hunters: A group comprised solely of Born vampires whose sole purpose is to hunt down any vampire that has broken the law, and either bring them to justice or execute them.

Incubus: A creature of seduction, built for the sole purpose of coupling with female humans to create new Born vampires. If an Incubus falls in love, they develop a distinctive scent.

Lycans: The product of a Primal werewolf and human female union. They can shift into a wolf whenever they like.

Primal werewolves: Originally human men who have been scratched by a succubus, turning them to a werewolf when the full moon rises.

The Bicus plane: A mystical realm only accessible to those with the blood of the Bicus. Time moves differently inside the plane, moving slower or faster than Earth depending on the moment.

The Order Acilino: Location in Spain, name translates to "Eagle."

The Order Bête: Location in Canada, name translates to "Beast."

The Order Dedliwan: Location in Australia, name translates to "Deadly."

The Order Engel: Location in Greenland, name translates to "Angel."

The Order Gennadi: Location in Russia, name translates to "Noble."

The Order Janiccat: Location in Malaysia, name translates to "Born."

The Order Khalid: Location in Algeria, name translates to "Immortal."

The Order Oleander: Location in the United States, name translates to "Poisonous."

The Order Qiángdù: Location in China, name translates to "Strength."

The Order Raposa: Location in Brazil, name translates to "Fox."

The Order Safed: Location in India, name translates to "Undamaged."

The Order Sangre: Location in Mexico, name translates to "Blood."

The turned vampires: Vampires that used to be humans and have been. Note: the word "turned" in reference to this type of vampire is never capitalized, hence referring to them as "the turned" to avoid this. They cannot turn humans, or give birth. The turned must drink human blood every day. Unlike the Born vampires, the turned vampires can survive on bagged blood.

Vaewolf: The product of a Primal werewolf or Lycan and a vampire union. They can shift into a wolf whenever they like, they have vampire fangs, and they require blood to heal if they are seriously injured. They do not require daily blood like vampires do.

Vipyre: The product of an Incubus and vampire female union. An incredibly rare creature, only one has ever been known to exist, but it is most likely due to lost knowledge as these creatures have been written about in Incubi lore.

Bathory Family

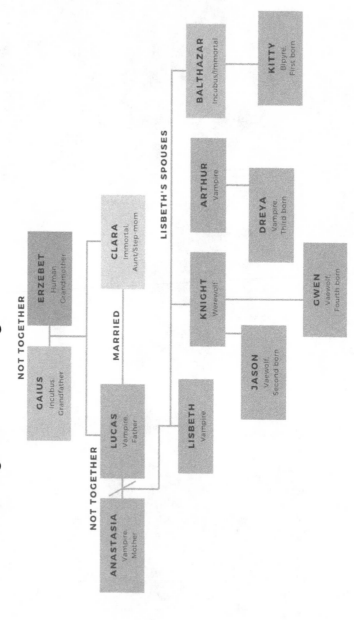

NOT TOGETHER

GAIUS
Incubus,
Grandfather

ERZEBET
Human,
Grandmother

CLARA
Immortal,
Aunt/Step-mom

MARRIED

NOT TOGETHER

ANASTASIA
Vampire,
Mother

LUCAS
Vampire,
Father

LISBETH
Vampire

LISBETH'S SPOUSES

JASON
Vaewolf,
Second born

KNIGHT
Werewolf

GWEN
Vaewolf,
Fourth born

ARTHUR
Vampire

DREYA
Vampire,
Third born

BALTHAZAR
Incubus/Immortal

KITTY
Bipyre,
First born

Castle of the Order Oleander

Road to town

Front gate

Underground Garage ramp

Social Area

Life-sized Chessboard

Picnic Tables

Back gate

Christiania River

ABOUT THE AUTHOR

Photo by Elizabeth Dunlap

Elizabeth Dunlap is the author of several fantasy books, including the Born Vampire series. She's never wanted to be anything else in her life, except maybe a vampire. She lives in Texas with her boyfriend, their daughter, and a very sleepy chihuahua named Deyna.

You can find her online at
www.elizabethdunlap.com

CPSIA information can be obtained
at www.ICGtesting.com
Printed in the USA
LVHW090407261120
672678LV00003BB/473